THE BIRTH OF RONIN

SUMMONED TO ANOTHER WORLD AND FORCED TO
FIGHT THE DEMON KING
BOOK TWO

JAMES E. WISHER

SAND HILL PUBLISHING

Edited by: Janie Linn Dullard

Cover art by: B-Ro

050520251.0

CHAPTER 1

D anny's stomach snarled at him as he marched steadily southeast. His clothes were filthy and he itched everywhere. He was sticking to the road in the hope that it would lead him to a town where he could get supplies and a bath. His lack of money was a minor problem, one easily dealt with by stealing whatever he needed. Any goodwill he'd harbored for the people of this world had died along with the hero. For now, only his survival mattered, and if anyone should get in his way, that was their bad luck.

A day had passed since he came back to life only to discover his companions had buried him six feet underground. He'd been surprised by that, though why he'd been surprised he couldn't say. Generally, dead bodies got buried. Or cremated. What would've happened if they'd decided to burn his body just in case? He didn't know, but a certain morbid curiosity made him wonder.

Would his wish have built him a new body? Given the power of the spell, he assumed so. After all, it couldn't bring him back to life as a pile of ash.

He glanced at the shadows. His best guess was three hours remained until dark. Another night without food, sleeping under the stars, didn't appeal to him.

Grinding his teeth in annoyance, Danny picked up the pace. He didn't know exactly how far he had to go to reach the capital but on foot he assumed a couple of weeks. Part of him wanted to get there as soon as possible while another part wanted to savor the journey as he anticipated his reunion with the elf-blood bitch who murdered him. Lyra Shael would suffer for her betrayal, Danny swore it.

"Well, well, what do we have here?" Half a dozen men even dirtier than Danny emerged from the trees on the side of the road. They held a mix of clubs and shortswords and were all grinning like idiots.

Danny had been so preoccupied by his thoughts he didn't even notice them. Pathetic. He needed to get his head on straight or he wouldn't live long enough to get his revenge.

"Don't look like he's got anything worth taking," a different bandit said.

"His clothes look pretty nice," a third one said. "Once we wash them we can get a few coins for them."

The first bandit, the biggest of the lot at a hair over six feet tall, slapped his club into the palm of his hand. "You want to strip naked for us or do we kill you and strip your corpse? I'm good with either."

"I've already been killed once this week," Danny said. "Can't say I'm interested in dying again."

When the bandits looked at each other in confusion, Danny called the ether.

Lightning blasted from his fingertips, arcing from bandit to bandit as it burned holes through their chests. In a few seconds the road was quiet again. Steam rose from the charred corpses. After demons and ogres, a handful of filthy bandits didn't pose much of a challenge.

Danny patted them down but came up with nothing. Hardly a surprise. Anyone desperate enough to rob someone as poor looking as Danny had to be in a rough spot. Maybe they had a camp around here.

He opened himself fully to the ether and let his senses expand. A minute later he caught a whiff of smoke. Someone had a fire going. A fire often meant food. Curious and optimistic, Danny followed the scent off the road and into the woods. A fifteen-minute walk brought him to the edge of a clearing where a small campfire burned in a circle of stones. A single figure sat on a wooden trunk beside it drinking from a bronze mug. He was just as dirty as the bandits, but the broadsword beside him looked polished and well cared for.

"Are you going to stand there staring at my back all night or are you going to step into the clearing so we can talk?" the bandit asked.

Danny had been pretty quiet though he hadn't bothered with magical stealth. How had the bandit known he was there? On this world, it was probably best to assume some sort of magic was involved. That being the case, Danny activated a number of defensive spells. Better safe than sorry after all.

Preparations made, he took another step into the clearing. "You should be careful. I ran into some bandits out on the road a minute ago. They might have smelled your fire."

The big man got to his feet in one smooth, graceful motion before collecting his sword and turning to face Danny. "Those were my men, but I guess you figured that out already. Since you're here and they aren't, can I assume they're dead?"

"They tried to rob me, so I didn't have much choice. Since you're the leader of the group, I fear I have to hold you partially responsible for your underlings' actions."

"You should've kept walking, stranger. See, I was an arcane knight before the demon king showed up. Decided to desert rather than let a demon kill me. Being a bandit's not much of a life, but at least I survived."

The bandit lunged and slashed at high speed.

Danny saw through the attack and caught the blade six inches from his neck. The edge of a normal weapon had no hope of cutting through his personal shield.

The bandit stared at him, dumbfounded.

"You're right. With skills like those you wouldn't have lasted long against a demon." Lightning arced down the length of the sword and into the bandit, who spasmed before collapsing in front of Danny, somehow still alive. "I'm impressed you survived that spell."

The former knight twitched as his muscles clenched and locked. Danny flipped the sword once and caught it by the hilt. It wasn't the hero's sword by any means, but it would serve for now. He pointed at the bandit and a second lightning bolt finished what the first started.

When he sensed no more life force, Danny bent and patted the dead man down. This time he had better luck, coming up with a handful of silver coins, the small ones, about the size of a dime back home. Not a fabulous fortune, but hopefully enough to get him a room and a meal should he ever have the good luck to reach a village.

Leaving the corpse where it lay, he went to the trunk. An iron padlock was hooked through the latch, but not closed tight. He flipped it aside and opened the lid. Alas, no heap of gold and jewels greeted him. Instead he found three pairs of leather boots, a decent green cloak, a satchel, and a sheathed dagger. No doubt these were the spoils from the group's victories. That they'd had any victories impressed Danny. Maybe their leader fought with them occasionally. Though no match for Danny, he would've been trouble for the average traveler.

He opened the satchel and grinned. Dried crackers and jerky. Not a feast by any means, but he wasn't about to complain. On the far side of the trunk he found a half-full skin of ale as well as the sheath and baldric for the bandit's sword.

Provisions in hand, Danny settled in for a bite to eat.

Getting the dried food down was harder work than killing the bandits, but his body was grateful for the sustenance. When he finished, Danny put the remaining food back into the satchel. He still had a few hours of daylight and hoped to reach a village before dark. He took the dagger and cloak out of the trunk. The boots he had no use for.

Now somewhat properly equipped and with a few coins in his pocket, Danny set out again. Leaving the forest behind, he turned down the road. The food had energized him and he was eager to make some time. Finding a former knight had been unexpected, but apparently every world had cowards and deserters. It was probably a universal thing. Wherever you had people you'd have good ones and bad ones.

He kept his senses alert as he jogged along. Letting his angry thoughts distract him was foolish. Anger in general was a useless emotion. Much as he wanted payback, it was only a temporary motivator. He had his whole life ahead of him, so finding a reason to live it was important.

Shaking off the distraction, he focused on the job at hand. This was still dangerous territory. Even though he'd killed the demon king, or queen in this case, there still had to be a lot of demons and monsters wandering around. Danny got damn lucky a bunch of weakling humans ambushed him instead of a squad of blackguards. Given his current equipment, he seriously doubted he'd have any chance of beating one of the dark warriors, much less a handful.

An hour before sunset, Danny sensed the familiar darkness of demonic corruption, and not far away. He charged his sword with holy energy and increased the power to his personal shield before continuing on, every sense alert for danger.

When he crested a hill, he spotted the source of the corruption. A village was under attack. He picked out a pair of hellhounds, as well as a trio of the lamprey-headed monsters. Not a particularly strong force, but more than enough to deal with a backwater village.

He hesitated for only a moment before rushing into battle. He could've kept his distance and let the demons have their way with the village then gone in and taken whatever he needed for his journey. Part of him was tempted, but in the end, these people weren't his enemy and Danny didn't have it in him to look away when others were in danger. Sometimes he wished he did, but he wasn't wired that way.

Turning his physical enhancement up to about ninety percent, he kicked off and sprinted into battle.

A hellhound spotted him first. It barely turned before Danny disintegrated it with a holy lance. A moment later the head of a lamprey demon went flying. His new sword didn't cut anything like the hero's sword, but enhanced with holy energy it was enough to deal with small fry like these.

He grimaced as he went looking for more enemies. Danny wasn't the hero anymore. If he acted like killing demons was simple, people would ask uncomfortable questions. There weren't many arcane knights capable of defeating five demons on their own. In fact, he was pretty sure Lyra was the only one with that much power.

He spotted the second hellhound chasing down a family of three who were running for all they were worth. The demon could've caught them at any time, but the monster seemed to be enjoying their fear. A second holy lance erased the demon from reality.

Maybe it would make him stand out, but damned if he was going to let those bastards have their way.

Between his magical senses and the screams, it was easy to locate the last two demons. Since a group of villagers was watching, Danny made it look like the fight was harder than it really was before finishing them off.

He let his senses drift across the village, but found no more corruption. For the moment, the area was secure.

His new sword was coated with gore and blood despite the magical aura he'd used to enhance 'it. He got busy burning it off with holy light. As he worked, one of the villagers he'd rescued, an older man around forty dressed in a tattered tan tunic and trousers, moved hesitantly closer. The rest stayed huddled together while watching him with nervous eyes.

"Excuse me, sir," the spokesman said. "Many thanks for the rescue. I feared we were going to be wiped out. Are you an adventurer?"

Danny wasn't sure how to respond, so he went with a

heavily edited version of the truth. "No, sir. Not yet. I was on my way to the capital when I sensed the demons. I'm glad I was able to help."

"You did more than help, young man," he said. "Our weapons, such as they are, couldn't even scratch those things. You dealt with them as easily as I might a misbehaving child."

"Hopefully you wouldn't be that hard on a child." Danny grinned. "I was studying with a retired arcane knight. The plan was to join the army and fight the demon king's forces, but I got word that the hero had defeated the demon king so I went to plan B, joining the Adventurers' Guild. If you're going to fight demons, might as well get paid for it."

The villager nodded like he believed Danny's story. Whether he did or not, at least he wasn't asking uncomfortable questions. The people behind him had relaxed a fraction as well.

"You don't need to go to the capital to join the guild," the villager said. "There are branches at all the bigger towns and cities. Not ours unfortunately."

"I know," Danny said despite not having a clue. "But I'm also going to visit an old friend in the capital. Two birds with one stone as my teacher always says. Would it be possible for me to stay here for the night? A hot meal wouldn't go amiss either."

"Of course, that's the least we can offer considering what you've done for us. My name is Val and I'm the headman of this village. You're welcome to stay in my home."

Danny bowed. "I appreciate your generosity. My name is Ronin and I am at your service."

Where the hell did that name come from? It had just popped into Danny's head, so he used it. Not many people knew the hero's real name, but he figured it was best not to use it anymore. Ronin would serve as well as any other.

Val got busy shouting orders to clean up the village and collect the bodies for burning, then he led Danny to a modest house with three rooms and a thatch roof. It was nothing fancy, but beat sleeping under the stars. After a meal of soup and bread, Danny settled on the floor of the main room.

Though he was tired and full, he found sleep slow in coming. Helping the villagers had felt good. He'd had no plan to become an adventurer, but maybe that would be a better path. Revenge, satisfying as it might have been, wasn't useful. He was a soldier and he'd sworn an oath to protect the Alliance. All the hero business had made him lose track of his duty. There was still a way he could protect his old world, and Lyra would be the one to help him figure out how to do it.

She owed him that at the very least.

CHAPTER 2

High Priestess Eve Carre knelt in front of Adonael's altar in the Crystal Cathedral. She prayed to her patron with total devotion, not for any particular answer but rather for reassurance. Her heart had been troubled since Daniel's death fighting the demon king. She knew it could happen of course. Considering it had already happened five times, the odds of his survival were painfully low. But still, her heart said she should've been able to do something to prevent it.

She looked up at the altar. The white cloth covering it was pristine and Adonael's halo on the front seemed to shine with an inner light. Last Holy Day people had packed the cathedral to bursting, all giving thanks for the hero's victory. They didn't even know his name. That struck her as wrong. Daniel wasn't just a symbol, he was a person.

At last she sighed and got to her feet. Looked like today wasn't going to be the day Adonael answered her doubts.

In addition to summoning the hero, the cathedral served another important purpose. There was a special chamber near the back which allowed Eve to survey the level of corruption in the Five Kingdoms. She needed to check it before her meeting with King Richard. Nearly a month had passed since Daniel's victory and the level of corruption had yet to drop back to the pre-attack level. According to the histories she'd read, it should only take two weeks to get back to normal.

Eve didn't know what it meant and that worried her. Of course, everything worried her lately. With a little shake of her head, she left the chapel and worked her way deeper into the cathedral. Only members of the faith were allowed in here. They weren't hiding any secrets or anything, but the tremendous flow of ether sometimes made people unused to it ill. Only Adonael's grace had allowed Eve to withstand it when she first arrived.

Golden energy ran through the walls, sparkling like fireflies. She slid a hand across the cool surface. The people's prayers charged the building with energy and it took a hundred years to build up enough to trigger the summoning ritual. Eve thanked Heaven that only two more heroes would need to be summoned. Two more lives cut short to ensure five thousand years of peace. A small price for the greater good. Eve wished she could convince herself that was the truth.

She stopped in front of a particular section of wall, summoned ether into her finger, and made the halo symbol over her head. The wall vanished and she stepped into a small, square room. It was completely empty and served only as a way to enhance Eve's ability to sense corruption. The pure energy filling the air also served as insulation to protect her mind when she touched the darkness.

Easing down to the hard floor, she centered herself and

opened her awareness to the world. She focused northwest, toward Demon King Castle. As soon as she did, the dark wall of Fell Forest slammed into her awareness. The corruption remained so strong. It had only decreased by a quarter at most. The castle itself looked like a dark fountain in the ether, blackening everything as it spewed corruption.

It was so wrong. The output was still double what it should be. King Richard would not be best pleased by the news. The constant raids on outlying villages and towns were wearing him down and he was quick to bark at anyone bringing more ill news. When she updated him at the meeting this afternoon, it would likely be Eve's turn to get barked at.

She started to draw her awareness back to her body, then something grabbed her and soon she was flying upwards. It didn't feel evil, so she let it take her. A moment later she stood among white clouds. A golden gate glowed in the distance. A light appeared directly in front of her and took the shape of a beautiful, if stern, woman. She wore a white robe and white feathered wings jutted from her back. A golden halo hung over her head.

"Adonael." Eve tried to kneel but found she couldn't move.

"I must be brief," the archangel said. "The hero failed to fully purify the demon king. The cycle isn't over."

"What—"

"I dare say no more lest it be considered a breach of the contract I made with the demon lords."

Eve blinked and found herself back in the focusing chamber. She didn't know what to think. If the demon king survived and the hero didn't, how would the Five Kingdoms win? And where was the demon king now? So many questions and so few answers. One thing she did know for sure: the king needed to be told at once. What he could do about it was another matter, one she'd worry about later.

She scrambled to her feet and hurried out. This news wouldn't keep until the meeting.

○

Lyra hated visiting Villipan Castle. She'd always hated it, but usually her presence wasn't required between cycles. Unfortunately, things weren't remotely usual right now. Demons and monsters beyond counting were scattered around the Five Kingdoms, causing havoc. New reports from military patrols came in daily and the news was never good. Farms burned, villages destroyed, fields corrupted beyond use—it was a nightmare. The other kings had returned to their respective capitals and the few reports they'd sent indicated that matters were no better elsewhere.

The guards hardly even looked at her as she passed through the castle gate. She'd been visiting daily in the hope of helping come up with a solution to the current crisis. Unfortunately they all knew the only solution: kill the monsters roaming the countryside. She knew it, the king knew it, and the general knew it. Discussing the matter was pointless, yet discuss it they would for many tedious hours.

"Lady Shael!"

Lyra paused a few feet inside the gate and let Eve join her. The red-faced priestess looked like she'd run all the way from the cathedral. They still had an hour before the meeting, so what brought her here in such haste?

"Eve, you're looking worked up. Is all well?"

"No, all is not well." Eve looked at the guards then back. "I need to talk to you and the king, privately if at all possible."

Lyra knew the priestess well enough to recognize the panic she was barely keeping under control. Whatever had happened, it was serious. "Richard wanted to talk to me before the meeting. Some new plan to speed the hunt. It'll likely be of no more use than all the others, but I have to listen anyway. You can come along and share your news. I'm assuming it pertains to the problem at hand."

"It definitely does. Thank you."

Lyra nodded and started walking again. She hadn't done anything worthy of thanks, but perhaps taking a bit of the weight off Eve's shoulders had been enough.

As they crossed the courtyard Eve asked, "Are you holding up okay? You spent more time with Daniel than any of us. I'm sure his death hit you the hardest."

Lyra nearly flinched at the question. The most recent hero seldom entered her thoughts and on those occasions when he did, she made a point of banishing him quickly. He was not a subject she wanted to discuss with Eve.

"This may sound harsh to you," Lyra said. "But I've seen so many humans die over my fifteen hundred years that I'm hardly bothered anymore. Your lives are like flickering flames snuffed out in a blink. Daniel's burned brighter than most for his brief time on our world. We should honor him but not dwell on it."

"I hadn't considered it from your point of view before," Eve said. "It must be difficult, living amongst people with such short lifespans."

Lyra wanted few things less than she wanted Eve's sympathy. "*Life* is difficult and I do what I must to keep my people safe."

At the keep entrance the guards opened the heavy doors for them. As soon as they entered, Lyra headed straight for the royal residence. The only positive thing to happen over the past month was Alban Morel and his knights getting deployed out of the city. Not having the fool of a noble underfoot came as a huge relief.

The halls were mobbed as servants and messengers came and went. The slap of their footsteps wore on Lyra's nerves. Humans were such noisy creatures. Everyone hastened to make way for Lyra and Eve; one of the privileges of high rank.

At last they reached the royal suite and the blessed quiet that came with it. Lyra knocked and a moment later Richard's gruff voice said, "Come in."

Lyra pulled the door open and strode through with Eve on her heels. The king was seated at the dining table, alone as she'd expected. His hard, narrow gaze shifted to Eve. "I thought I said I wanted to speak with you alone."

"It's my fault, Majesty," Eve said. "I received an oracle from Adonael and needed to tell you about it right away."

This news surprised even Lyra. The archangel hadn't given an oracle since before the first demon king. Whatever news she felt compelled to share, it had to be bad.

The wrinkles in Richard's brow grew even deeper as he glowered. "Very well, tell me."

"Adonael says Daniel didn't fully purify the demon king. She's still alive somewhere and that's likely why the level of corruption hasn't returned to normal."

Lyra's jaw dropped. Nothing else Eve could've said would've shocked her more. She'd seen the deaths of six demon kings and they all looked exactly like what happened this time. The black pillar was the same, the castle doors closing, the same, everything was the same.

And then she understood. It was the perfect trick. If you make everything look the same, no one would question what really happened. If Ardent Lilly knew about what Lyra did to the previous heroes, it would make perfect sense to pretend the hero had won, let Lyra strike the final blow, then have the demon king come back with no one to oppose her. It was brilliant, in a horrifying way.

"What else did Adonael say?" Richard asked.

"Nothing, Majesty. Other than that to say more would risk the contract she'd made with the demon lords. I assume if she breaks it, that would negate all humanity has done this past fifteen hundred years and the demon lords would be free to make another all-out assault on our world."

"This is not the news I was hoping for," Richard said. "Is it safe to assume that the demon king is still guiding the creatures attacking my people?"

"We can assume it if you like," Lyra said. "But the truth is it doesn't matter. Guided by the demon king or not, the demons still need to be hunted down, and the sooner the better. The dark pillar I saw likely carried her body somewhere safe to recover. No doubt somewhere far from the Five Kingdoms. This demon king is smart. She'll bide her time, build an even bigger force, and eventually return and march all the way to the cathedral. And worst of all, we have no one capable of stopping her this time."

"It can't be hopeless," Eve said. "Why would Adonael even bother to give me an oracle if we had no chance of victory?"

Lyra shook her head. That was a good question. Unfortunately, she had no answers.

"Thank you, Eve, for bringing this important news to our

attention," Richard said. "I trust you know not to let anyone outside this room know what you've learned."

"Or course, Majesty. If word of the demon king's survival got out, the panic would be tremendous."

Richard stood and walked over to Eve, gently guiding her toward the door. "Exactly. I knew I could count on your wisdom. Please, should Adonael have anything else to say, bring the news to me at any time, day or night."

"I will," Eve said. "Is there anything else I can do to help?"

Richard opened the door. "You can be a beacon of light for the people, as you have been. And you can pray for us."

"I will, Majesty. Do you wish me to remain for the meeting?"

"Given the new information you've provided, I think we'll postpone the meeting until tomorrow. I hope you'll join us then, same time as today."

She offered a little bow. "Of course."

Richard closed the door and rounded on Lyra. She put a sound barrier in place before he spoke. "How could you possibly have failed me this badly? If that girl is correct, and, while I have my doubts about her competence in general, I'm pretty sure she wouldn't mistake a divine message for something else, how in Adonael's name are we going to win?"

"I have no answers for you, Majesty," Lyra said. "Nothing like this has ever happened. We find ourselves in wholly uncharted waters. For now, I suggest we focus on dealing with the enemies at hand. If the demons kill everyone, it won't matter what the demon king does when she returns."

"That is not overly helpful."

She shrugged. Panicking would do no one any good. Though, even if she remained calm on the outside, on the inside, Lyra was as close to panicking as she'd ever been.

"That's the best advice I can offer at this time. We need more information. Until we get it, there's nothing any of us can do."

Richard ground his teeth but nodded. "So be it. When we're finished with the generals tomorrow, I want you to return to Demon King Castle. Figure out where the demon king went. You're our best fighter and she's bound to be weakened after her fight with the hero. Hunt her down and finish what he started."

Lyra knew from the tone of his voice that the king would accept no arguments. She didn't have high hopes for success, but it couldn't hurt to take another look around. There might be a clue somewhere.

Though if this demon king was as smart as she feared, the odds of success didn't bear thinking about.

CHAPTER 3

Not long after noon, Danny stood outside the hero's mansion and stared at the beautiful, sprawling building. The stone looked as smooth as the day it was built and someone had recently given it a fresh coat of whitewash, probably the same elf-bloods who maintained the gardens. There had been a time not so long ago that he thought he might live out his days here. Lyra's granddaughters were sweet kids and he found their innocence charming. It would've been nice to watch them grow up. Peaceful.

His walk here had been far from peaceful. After saving that first village, he'd accepted supplies as payment and set out. Three times he'd been forced to slaughter groups of demons. They were weak things, no match for the hero. But their presence made it clear that defeating the demon king had done little to improve the situation on the ground.

Well, once he officially became an adventurer he could make some good coin hunting them down. Or so he hoped. His funds were painfully low and he suspected he'd need a great deal more to fund his travels for his ultimate plan to have any hope of success.

But first things first. He needed his ring. Opening himself fully to the ether, he examined the wards surrounding the mansion. They were quite strong. No surprise given who made them. But quite strong and strong enough to stop him were two different things.

Danny formed ether into a hammer the size of a wagon and slammed it into the barrier. Cracks spiderwebbed through the spell. A second blow spread them further. The third sent the collected energy back where it came from.

He wiped sweat from his brow and walked up to the door. Naturally, it was locked. A flick of the ether remedied that problem and he pulled it open. Okay, first things first. Expanding his senses, he located his ring. The magic was bound to his soul; no one had the power to hide it from him. Next he located the girls' life forces. They must have heard him as they were running his way.

Not terribly wise to run toward an intruder.

Danny activated his stealth field and moved silently away from the door. He didn't have to wait long before two little dark-haired elf girls came barreling into the entryway. They stared at the open door and as they did, Danny hit them both with a paralysis spell. They went rigid and he caught them with a telekinesis spell before they fell. Very gently he closed their eyes and muffled their ears.

He looked down at the unconscious children. Nothing he could do would hurt Lyra more than killing these two. When he first climbed out of his grave, had they been in front of him, he might have strangled them both. Fortunately for the girls, he'd had time to think, and more importantly calm down. Their deaths would improve nothing. Better for the world if they grew up safe and happy.

Using his magic, he carried the pair up to their room and put them to bed. His spell would last for a couple of hours, plenty of time to do what he had to.

Now for his ring. Following the connection down to Lyra's room, he opened the door and stepped inside. Aside from a dresser and bed, the room was empty. It might have been a room at an inn for all the personality it showed. Danny wasn't sure what that said about Lyra. Probably nothing good.

His ring rested on top of the dresser in a little glass bowl. And it wasn't alone. Six others kept it company. She was like a serial killer keeping trophies. He plucked his out of the bowl and slipped it onto his right hand. As soon as he channeled ether through it, the linked pocket dimension opened. He reached in and pulled out the ethersword's mithril hilt. His new sword had served him well, but it felt good to hold the ethersword once more.

"Tara! Nora!" A terrified voice shouted from downstairs. The mistress of the house had returned.

Danny reactivated his stealth field, including invisibility, and got ready for his reunion.

○

Lyra massaged her forehead as General Gaul read the most recent reports. The numbers were depressing. Hundreds more killed across the Five Kingdoms. The details didn't matter terribly much. To prove it, no one bothered to mark the locations of each attack on the war room map. The fact that they'd run out of black pins likely had something to do with it as well.

Beside her, Eve looked sick. A perfectly understandable reaction. At least she hadn't brought any more news from Adonael. They needed more bad news like they needed a plague. From his seat at the head of the table, Richard looked far older than his forty-five years. Lyra had a pretty good idea how he imagined the post-victory cleanup would go and this wasn't it.

At last the general said, "That concludes the reports on new fatalities. I will now read the commanders' reports from our combat patrols."

He took a breath just as a sharp pain stabbed Lyra in the temple. Someone had broken through the ward at the hero's mansion. Only a powerful demon possessed the strength to manage such a thing.

She leapt to her feet. "I have to go."

"Sit down!" Richard said. "We're in the middle of the meeting."

"Someone breached the mansion's wards. The girls might be in danger. I'm going." With that she raced for the exit.

Lyra ran through the castle, dodging around humans who were too slow to get out of her way. Moments later she was through the outer wall and sprinting through the streets toward the western gate. Wide-eyed people stared at her but she had no time for them.

When she reached the gate, it was down. Gathering ether in her legs, she sprang over the wall, landed lightly beside a wagon laden with squash, and ran on.

She encountered no one else on her way and soon the mansion was in sight. She sensed no corruption. Any demon

THE BIRTH OF RONIN

capable of defeating her ward should've been easy to detect. Perhaps it had killed the girls and moved on.

No! She refused to believe it.

Lyra burst through the unlocked door, sword in hand. "Tara! Nora!"

No response and still no aura of corruption. She relaxed a fraction when she sensed two strong life forces. Bounding up the stairs, she reached the girls' room in seconds.

A long sigh escaped her. They were lying in bed, unharmed. She looked closer. Some sort of magical aura surrounded them.

She gathered ether to dispel it.

"Let them rest," a familiar, impossible voice said. "We have a great deal to discuss."

She spun and watched Daniel shimmer into view. He held a lit ethersword in his right hand. Lyra couldn't decide which was more impossible, his survival or that he held one of the rarest elven artifacts.

"Daniel. How are you..."

"Alive? That's an interesting story. The short version is, after I freed Merrok—that's the fire drake—from the demon's control, he was grateful. We chatted a bit and he gave me two gifts. This excellent sword is one and a star ring was the other."

"How did the drake come to possess two of the ancient elves' greatest treasures?" Lyra could hardly believe it. In fact, if she weren't seeing the results of a wish right in front of her, she would've said all the star rings had been long since used up.

"He didn't say and we didn't have very long to talk. The corruption was killing him quickly." Daniel shook his head, seeming a little sad. "I wanted to use the wish to kill the demon king, but he assured me that was impossible due to Ardent Lilly's protection. So I used it to resurrect myself should I be killed. Though I assumed the demon king would kill me, not you."

Lyra flinched at the coldness in his voice. It didn't surprise her, but it hurt all the same. His survival might end up being the best thing that could've happened. What were the odds of both the demon king and the hero living through the final battle? This had to be why Adonael sent her oracle.

"I need to tell you something," Lyra said. She spoke in a calm, even tone, like nothing had happened between them.

"I don't care what you have to tell me," Daniel said. "I came here for my ring—nice collection you have of them, by the way—and for information. Whatever problems you have, they're no longer anything to do with me."

Lyra frowned. "What information do you want? Maybe we can make a deal."

"What sort of deal?"

"I'll answer your question and in exchange you promise to listen to what I have to say."

Daniel shrugged and nodded. "That's fine. Tell me how your ancestors linked our worlds."

"That's what you want to know? Why?" she asked.

"Just answer the question."

"The truth is I don't know. The half-elves of the High Council completed the magic not long after I was born. I was far too young to understand, though I remember everyone being excited when it happened. How stupid they all were. If only they hadn't been so arrogant, none of this would've been necessary. But, hindsight, as they say."

Daniel ground his teeth. "If you can't tell me, then who can?"

"No one living, you can be sure. Now it's my turn."

"Why should I listen? You told me nothing of any value." He turned to leave.

"Wait!"

Somewhat to her astonishment, he stopped and turned back. "What?"

"The survivors of the Reaper's reprisal brought some books with them. They're in the castle library for safekeeping. They may say something of value. I don't know."

He blew out a long sigh. "Fine. Say what you have to."

"Eve received an oracle from Adonael. The demon king survived your battle. The corruption in Fell Forest isn't dropping like it should. Our working theory is that she's biding her time, regaining her strength for another assault."

Daniel nodded. "So that's what she meant. I admit when she told me killing her wouldn't solve the world's problems, I thought she was being philosophical rather than literal. Well, good for her. Was there anything else?"

"What do you mean is there anything else? If the demon king is still alive, your duty as the hero—"

Sharp, bitter laughter cut her off. "Stop, just stop. You can't possibly imagine I'd help you now. And if you did, that makes you stupider than your ancestors who invaded my world. I'm going to give you one warning. Stay out of my way. I have no pity or mercy left for you and your masters. Get in my way and I'll kill you."

Daniel deactivated his ethersword and faded from sight. Lyra couldn't even sense his presence. She sat on the edge of the girls' bed, her legs unable to hold her. When she first saw him, she'd thought it was fate that let him survive. Now she knew better. The Five Kingdoms were truly on their own.

CHAPTER 4

An hour after sunset Danny approached Castle Villipan. The streets were empty and the only noise came from open taverns. There was music, laughter, and light. The trouble in the countryside wasn't keeping the city folk from enjoying themselves. No, that wasn't fair. He doubted the average person had any idea what was happening beyond the walls. When winter arrived and food became scarce, then reality would set in.

He felt bad for them, but Danny was determined not to get involved with the royals and military. He didn't mind killing demons and monsters, and the people living in the small, defenseless villages seemed to appreciate his help.

He gave a sad shake of his head and focused on the task at hand. The librarian should still be on duty at this hour. If anyone would know where to find the books he needed, she would.

Invisible and silent, he reached the castle wall. The portcullis was down and no guards were visible outside.

That was fine. He hadn't intended to go through the gate anyway. A magic enhanced leap carried him up and over the wall. An owl would've made more noise than he did. Danny noticed wall guards in passing, but they didn't react to him at all.

Small wonder the demons had no trouble making it into the castle. Even now, when he felt certain some of the wizards were back from the front, no one had placed any sort of magical alarm. He thought Lyra might've done it, but as far as he could tell, she didn't have much use for the humans who ran the kingdom. They kept her people safe and she killed their enemies. Certainly no love was lost.

He crossed the courtyard to the keep door and found it also closed with no guards visible outside. Getting in here would be trickier, but far from impossible. It would've been nice if the castle had normal-sized windows, but that would've been imprudent for a fortification.

Extending his awareness into the castle, he found a pair of guards just inside. Perfect. This would be a good chance to test his ability with psychic magic. Defending against it was simple as long as you were stronger than the person trying to manipulate you. Controlling someone else, on the other hand, took finesse, assuming you didn't want to leave them brain dead. While Danny would do what he had to, he'd gotten to like a number of the castle guards and had no interest in harming them.

Gently as he could, Danny reached out with the ether. The energy oozed into both guards' heads before soaking their brains. He felt the spell take hold; part one complete. Since magic worked mainly by visualizing what you wanted to happen, he focused on an image of the door opening. He didn't push too hard, but he also didn't let up. It took half a minute but finally the door swung open enough for him to slip inside.

The guards were staring straight ahead with vacant expressions. They looked a bit too zombified for comfort, but he put that out of his mind and ordered them to lock the door and return to their posts. He left the control spell lightly in place so he could reactivate it when he returned.

It didn't take long to make the walk to the library. The handful of guards and servants he passed didn't even flinch. Using a stealth field almost seemed unfair. Not that fairness interested him. All he cared about was getting what he needed and getting out of here unnoticed.

The usual woman stood behind the counter. Despite visiting the library several times he'd never gotten her name. Talking to the hero made her nervous and he figured the best thing he could do was leave as quickly as possible. She was reading something, not a surprise for a librarian. Danny didn't even bother getting closer. He activated the control spell again and just like with the guards, the librarian succumbed to his magic. The tricky part was, he didn't know exactly which books he needed which made it hard to visualize his order. With no better options he settled on "old books brought by the elves when they first arrived in Villipan."

Her eager compliance indicated that she knew what he wanted even if he didn't. She had barely disappeared into the stacks when an angry shriek filled the air followed by a woman screaming, "What part of 'stay at your desk until we leave' did you not understand?"

That sounded like Princess Claudette. Given her nature

Danny suspected it wasn't a reading session the librarian had interrupted.

Apologize and collect the books quickly. Danny sent the order speeding through their connection.

"Forgive me, Princess," the librarian said. "I'll be out of your way in a moment."

Danny started when he sensed someone approaching from the nobles' area. He'd been so focused on the altercation he hadn't noticed until the last second. He barely got out of the way in time to prevent Prince Florian from running into him.

What was this, a de Villipan family reunion?

"Claudette!" Florian shouted. "Are you here?"

The stomping of feet was followed by a red-faced Claudette emerging from the stacks as she tucked her left breast back into the top of her dress. "What? I was in the middle of someone."

"Father called a family meeting and sent me to find you. You can play hide the sausage with your new favorite later."

Claudette stopped a few feet away from Danny's hiding place. "What could possibly be so important that you had to come and get me personally?"

"Forte's capital has been sacked by a combined force of giants and demons. King Forte and his family barely escaped. Father wants to discuss our evacuation plans should something similar happen to Villipan."

Claudette snorted. "If Villipan City falls it won't matter where we go. Ours is the largest and strongest city in the Five Kingdoms."

"I don't disagree, but Father wants to talk and he's in one of his moods. The sooner we get back the sooner you can return to your fun." Florian turned to look at the library, or more specifically, the nervous-looking young man peeking out from behind a bookcase. "Couldn't you at least find someone with a spine to dally with?"

"My playmates don't need a spine. Other portions of his anatomy are more than adequate to make up for it." Claudette pointed at her lover. "You, my quarters, midnight. Don't keep me waiting."

Without another word, she and Florian marched off. A moment later the boy toy hurried past Danny, adjusting his pants as he went. After that little display, Danny felt like he both missed out and dodged a bullet.

He put the nobles out of his mind when he sensed the librarian approaching.

Put the books on the table and forget ever getting them.

She set four leather-bound books on the table and turned away, just as Danny wished her to. He snuck over, grabbed the books, and put them in his ring's storage dimension. From the library door, he ended the spell. She slumped for a moment, gave a little shake of her head, then started rubbing her temples. Satisfied that he hadn't done any permanent damage, Danny retraced his steps to the castle door.

As he walked, he considered the conversation between the royals. He never got a chance to meet the king of Forte—demons crashing the party that was supposed to happen at had made small talk difficult. The sacking of a capital city was a far bigger thing than wiping out a farming village. Both were terrible of course, but the scale of what it would take to defeat a walled city was so much greater.

Well, they had armies and wizards and knights; surely someone would figure it out. Danny had his own task to complete. The Five Kingdoms could take care of themselves.

Richard held his head in his hand as he sat at the dining room table in the royal suite. He didn't know how things kept getting worse. The final battle had come and gone. The demon king was supposed to be dead along with the hero. The Five Kingdoms should be busy rebuilding and bringing in the harvest. Instead he had an army's worth of monsters running around wreaking havoc, up to and including destroying a capital city.

To his right, Clara sat silently chewing her lower lip. His eldest daughter seldom spoke unless asked a direct question. She was quiet, demure, sweet natured, and beautiful. Generally everything you might want in a princess. She never caused him a moment of grief and he loved her all the more for that kindness.

Claudette, on the other hand, gave him nothing but problems. Florian fell somewhere in the middle. If only he was less arrogant, and stupid, his only son and heir might actually be of some use in the current crisis. As it was, Richard had to rely on his general and the various captains for everything. Not an entirely comfortable position to be in given the current state of the world.

Gentle hands massaged his shoulders. "You need to relax, dear. Getting all wound up isn't going to help. You need to be calm and sure. The people look to you to lead them through this crisis."

He reached up and touched his dear wife's hand. "Thank you, Cecile. Though relaxing is far easier said than done. I fear sooner rather than later Villipan will face the same fate as Forte. My only hope lies with Lyra. If she can figure out where the demon king has gone and finish what the hero started, we may have a chance."

The door opened and Florian and Claudette strode through.

"What's so important that you needed to ruin my evening fun?" Claudette asked.

"Did your brother not tell you about Forte?" Richard asked.

"He did. So what? We can't do anything about it. I assume the royal family will be coming to stay with us."

"Yes, Miles and his family are on their way along with a strong force of knights and wizards. Getting them to reinforce Villipan is the only good thing to come out of this debacle."

"That's not a bad idea," Florian said. "What if we had all the kings and their families along with a portion of their armies come here. The extra manpower would make Villipan unassailable. It would be a perfectly secure bastion."

"That might work," Richard said. "But there are two problems. One is feeding everybody. With our harvest issues, it'll be a wonder if we make it through the winter as it is. Two, the other kings won't abandon their capitals lightly. We discussed it after the gala and no one would even consider such a thing. It's a sign of weakness."

"That's so stupid," Claudette said. "Getting killed is also a sign of weakness. Are they not worried about that?"

"Not as worried as they should be, I think," Richard said. "But in their defense I will admit if our positions were reversed, I wouldn't be quick to leave Villipan either. Their decisions are what they are. What I wanted to discuss is our plan should the worst happen. The only truly safe place in the city is the Crystal Cathedral. It can't be destroyed by anyone save the demon king. If we have to flee, that's where we go."

"Will the food problem not be an even bigger issue there?" Florian asked.

"The priests' magic can handle feeding a modest group. It won't be easy, but we will have Adonael's protection. That will give us time to make plans." Richard wasn't sure what plans they'd be able to come up with under those circumstances, but he saw no point in saying so.

"That's it?" Claudette asked. "If the demons attack, run to the cathedral, got it. Can I go now?"

Richard swallowed a longsuffering sigh. His daughter clearly either didn't have a brain rattling around in her pretty head, something he knew to be false, or she didn't fully appreciate the size of the threat. And even if she did, Claudette would be of little enough help in a crisis.

"Yes, go. But remember what I said. It might mean the difference between life and death."

She waved over her shoulder as she left. No doubt off to meet one of her playthings. Cecile rubbed his shoulders harder and whispered, "Steady, dear. Should, Adonael forbid, the enemy show up at our doorstep, she'll come around. But let us hope it doesn't come to that."

Richard hoped with all his might it didn't.

"Where's Lyra anyway?" Florian asked.

"I hope preparing to leave for Demon King Castle. There was some trouble at the hero's mansion and she hasn't returned yet. Which is fine. If there was a problem, I assume she'd let me know. I ordered her to leave as soon as possible. If anyone can figure out what's going on, she can."

"You put too much faith in her, Father," Florian said. "Alban says she's unreliable and that we should depend more on the knights."

"Alban Morel is an idiot who happens to have an influential brother. I'd sooner take advice from the servant that cleans my chamber pot. Lyra, on the other hand, has served our kingdom for over a thousand years with loyalty and skill. All things considered, I have no trouble deciding whom to rely on."

"That's rather unkind, Father. I've always found Alban quite clever."

"I don't know who you've been hanging around with if Alban seems clever by comparison, but I suggest you find better friends. Are you prepared for the inspection tomorrow?"

"What's to prepare for, and for that matter, what's the point?" Florian asked. "Do you think our visiting will make the guards more alert?"

"I think that the common soldiers like to see their king and their future king taking an interest in them. These men put their lives on the line to protect us, son. Never forget that. A ruler's gravest responsibility is to spend the lives of his people wisely."

"I understand, Father. Rest assured, I'll be ready when the time comes."

Richard nodded and silently prayed that Florian would, indeed, be ready. "That's good, son. Off you go. Clara, you can return to your quarters as well if you wish."

When the royal siblings had taken their leave, Richard finally let out the sigh he'd been holding in. "He still has so much growing to do and hanging around with Alban Morel isn't speeding the process."

"Florian's a good boy," Cecile said. "Try to have a little faith."

Richard was trying his best to have faith. The problem was, every time his son spoke, that faith was undermined. They still had some time. Maybe not a lot, but hopefully enough.

CHAPTER 5

Danny couldn't afford the finest inn the city had to offer, but he did spring for a nice, clean room in a cheap, working-class part of the city. There was a bed, wardrobe, nightstand with a bowl and carafe of water, and of course, the ubiquitous chamber pot. Did indoor plumbing even exist in this world? If he ever found a place that had it, he might settle down permanently.

When he'd passed through the common room, he hardly drew a second glance. His battered, dirty clothes, worn green cloak, and scruffy beard marked him as nothing special. That was a much more comfortable place for Danny. All the attention and expectations of being the hero had been a strain on him. Better by far to be one of the guys. He scratched his head and grimaced. He hadn't washed in far too long. Given the state of hygiene in this world, the hair might have to go. It would also help disguise him.

Summoning ether into his hand, he rubbed it over his head and pictured his hair disintegrating. A few passes later and he had a smooth scalp. He grinned. Just like that day in basic when the barber shaved his head. He smiled at the nostalgic memory. Who would've ever thought he'd look back on basic with a smile.

Right, enough screwing around. He'd get something to eat later. The beef soup some of the patrons were enjoying looked very tempting. But first he wanted to take a look at his find. Somehow he doubted they'd be easy to read, but his host body knew a translation spell, so with any luck that would do the trick.

His storage space opened at his mental command and he pulled the books out. They were bound in leather and a faint aura surrounded them. He studied it for a moment before deciding it was some kind of preservation magic. Not an unreasonable precaution given their age. The main thing was that he saw no dangers in the spell.

Now for the translation magic. As with all magic it worked based on what he pictured. So Danny pictured the odd, angular squiggles on the cover of the first book shifting into English. The process was a bit like watching snakes dance but finally the cover read, History of the Elf-blood People Part 2.

Part two was a three-inch-thick book and two of the others weren't much smaller. Reading them was not going to be a speedy process. A quick bit of sorting confirmed that the history of the elven people ran for three volumes. The final book was only an inch thick and on the cover it said, Gazetteer of the Elven Empire. That looked promising.

He flipped it open and on the first page found a wonderfully detailed map of a huge landmass. Thankfully it had a scale on the side. One inch equaled about two thousand miles. Using his fingers, Danny measured the continent and found it was about twenty thousand miles across from east to west and fifteen thousand from north to south. On either side it was surrounded by ocean. He'd never imagined something so large. The Alliance was barely over three thousand miles across at its widest.

He scanned the map until he found Villipan. There was no Fell Forest and the kingdom was a single nation rather than a smaller part of the whole. It was interesting that the old kingdom had the same name as the current largest. Couldn't be a coincidence.

A quick scan of the map revealed deserts, forests, plains, several mountain ranges, and a lake about the size of the Mediterranean Sea. Scattered throughout the land were nations by the dozen, cities by the hundreds, and nothing about any magic capable of opening a portal between worlds. Though to be fair, the boss elves would certainly want such details kept on the down low.

He paged through it, reading names of kingdoms which probably no longer existed and of rulers a thousand-plus years dead. Halfway through his reading, the words started to get blurry as they shifted from English to Elvish and back. His concentration was wavering. Clearly the translation spell was one he'd have to use for a limited time.

He rubbed his eyes and closed the gazetteer before returning all the books to storage for safekeeping. He had time, and patience was a virtue. Best to get some dinner and sleep. He planned to leave Villipan City at first light and register at the Adventurers' Guild when he reached Rosenbar. Part of him wanted to make Villipan itself his base, just out of spite, but that would be foolish in the extreme.

He had a new mission now, he couldn't let his emotions get the better of him. Danny was determined to let no one else from Earth be killed to protect these ingrates. As a soldier, that was his duty.

◊

Despite his best intentions, Danny couldn't resist taking a quick look at the History of the Elf-Bloods volume one after dinner. The cook's biscuits sat like lead in his stomach and didn't encourage an early bedtime. He didn't miss much about life at the castle, but the food had been delicious. He pulled the book out of storage and settled down on his hard mattress.

The translation spell activated more easily this time and he started reading.

The story began with the true elves returning to Heaven. The reason for their coming as well as why they were recalled wasn't mentioned. Either it was a secret or the author simply didn't know. Given how long ago it happened, Danny figured it didn't really matter.

Once they were gone, some of their children, a group of eight half-elves chosen as the most powerful and wise, formed the High Council that would rule the elf-blood empire. An empire which spanned the entire continent. Having seen the map in the gazetteer, he was impressed. It made any empire on Earth look like nothing in comparison.

The elves didn't rule it directly. They had human and demi-human proxies who oversaw most of the provinces. It was easier that way and as long as the peace was maintained, they let the other races rule themselves as they wished. If ever two of the provinces got to fighting, the elves would come and put an end to it in short order, such was the potency of their magic.

There was some resentment among the other races, mostly those who desired to expand their territory but were prevented from doing so. Most of the people considered this a golden age where they had no need to worry about marauding armies coming to kill or enslave them. Monsters and beasts were a constant nuisance, but a manageable one.

Danny wasn't sure who the author of this history was, but he suspected it had to be an elf-blood. It was mostly written like a love letter to the ones in charge. Had a human written it, there would no doubt be a great deal more bitterness and resentment. How did the saying go? History was written by the winners.

He paged through a few chapters extolling the virtues of the High Council's leadership as well as the magical wonders the elf-bloods created in their forest capital.

Danny stopped and pulled the gazetteer out. A huge forest about two thousand miles west of Villipan was marked "Elfhome." Not exactly close by, but given the size of the continent it could've been worse. Assuming he couldn't find what he needed to know in these books, that would be a good target for more research.

He closed the gazetteer and got back to the history. It was mostly just more self-praise. Danny had no interest in it. The book ended with a cliffhanger. The half-elves of the council had discovered other worlds, one of which had a vastly different system of magic. The world was riven by war and international rivalry. If the elf-bloods went there and brought peace, the people would welcome them as heroes, maybe even gods. They would also have the chance to learn a new way to wield the ether, which would make them even more powerful. Visions of a world-spanning empire swam in their heads.

Danny frowned and closed the first book. Maybe it was written by a member of the council. How else could the author know what they were thinking? In any case, it sounded like the leaders got a little too full of themselves. Centuries of peace with no one around even close to strong enough to challenge your power would no doubt do bad things to your ego.

He rubbed his eyes, hesitated for only a moment, then pulled out book two.

It opened with a council meeting, pretty much confirming Danny's guess that the author was a member. Agreement was unanimous. They would go to rescue Earth and its people from themselves.

They started researching portal magic but quickly discovered that the amount of power necessary to travel to their chosen world was far too great for even the entire High Council combined to manage. They also lacked a source of mithril, so enhancing their magic was out. The most devout prayed to Heaven for a gift of the metal, but their devotion fell on deaf ears. Heaven was uninterested in helping them on their noble mission.

Danny chuckled to himself. Apparently it never occurred to the arrogant pricks to take the angels' silence as a sign that they were on the wrong path. Of course, Danny couldn't hold the angels blameless either. If they'd simply come right out and told the High Council to forget about Earth, it might have been enough to prevent the invasion. They tended to let the people of the mortal world do as they pleased, which was generally a good thing, but also had the potential to lead to tragedy.

Over a hundred years of research finally yielded a plan everyone felt confident would work. They would create a huge magical circle that would concentrate the world's ether into a single spell capable of connecting the two worlds.

Danny flipped the page, eager to see how the magic worked, and nearly threw the book across the room. All it said was that after two hundred years of effort the spell circle was completed. The elf-blood invasion force gathered in Elfhome and the portal opened.

He knew what happened during the war. Everyone learned about it in history class. The elves appeared first in Africa, where they built labs and began transforming the local wildlife into monsters to help them fight. They drove humanity to the brink of defeat before summoned demons turned the tide. Depending on the historian, some actually considered the Reaper a hero of humanity. Not many, and they were largely viewed as crackpots, but there were a few all the same. It said something about the size of the threat that anyone would think favorably of a demon lord.

From the elf-bloods' perspective, the people of Earth were a bunch of foolish savages too stupid to take advantage of their generosity. They were offered peace and order and instead they chose to fight. What happened next was an inevitable result of their poor decision. At least it was inevitable until the demons showed up. Their dark magic proved a poor mix for the elf-bloods' style of sorcery and they were steadily driven back until they had to flee the Earth altogether.

But that wasn't enough to satisfy the Reaper's rage. His followers on Valindor opened Hell portals and the Reaper sent his army through. The elves were slaughtered by the hundreds and driven out of Elfhome. It came close to being an extinction-level event for both sides, but at last Adonael stepped in and suggested a contest. The very contest which resulted in Danny's summoning.

His eyes were stinging so badly he finally had to stop. He'd made it through three books and while the history was interesting, it didn't provide any details about how to stop the magic from activating. Of course the one bit he absolutely needed to know was missing.

He returned all the books to storage and lay down. It had to be late. A ton of things had to happen before he could even think about heading for Elfhome, much less start unraveling the magic connecting Earth and Valindor. But he would figure it out. His host body was young and strong. Danny figured he had a good fifty years if he took care of himself. That should be enough time to finish his mission.

It would have to be. He swore to himself that no more innocent youths would die if he could help it.

CHAPTER 6

Danny slowly came awake to an awful pounding in his head. Maybe he'd used the translation spell for too long the night before. No, the pounding was coming from outside.

"Hey!" a disagreeable voice shouted. "If you're not out in fifteen minutes I'm charging you for another day."

He grimaced and opened his eyes. Danny hadn't needed a wakeup call since his second week in basic. The innkeeper had an even less pleasant voice than his drill sergeant, and he had sounded like he chewed nails and gargled gravel.

Given his travel plans and the lightness of his wallet, Danny rolled out of bed at once. The room didn't spin and his vision wasn't blurry. Those were both excellent indications that he hadn't overdone it too badly. The last thing he needed was one of those savage headaches he got during training, especially since Eve wasn't around to heal him.

He sighed. Danny wasn't sure how he felt about Eve. He doubted she was aware of Lyra's plans. She was too guileless to lie right to his face and make it believable. He doubted he'd see her again so his feelings didn't make much difference.

A quick splash of water on his face woke him the rest of the way up. He threw his clothes on and belted on his sword and dagger. Everything else he owned, and it wasn't much, was safe in storage. Ready to face the day, Danny pulled the door open and made the short walk to the stairs. The common room was empty and bright sunlight shone through the windows. His host stood behind the bar, hairy arms crossed, and a glower creasing his face.

"About time you got up."

Danny swallowed several nasty retorts. "I had a bad night's sleep. How much for a breakfast sandwich?"

"One small silver." The innkeeper's beady black eyes stared expectantly at Danny.

He dug a coin out of his pocket and slapped it on the bar. "Don't burn my toast."

The innkeeper grumbled and marched back into the kitchen. Ten minutes later he returned with a pale, sad-looking egg sandwich lacking both meat and cheese. Talk about a rip-off. But, whatever. Danny was hungry and in a hurry. It would do.

He took his depressing breakfast and left the inn with the firm conviction never to stay there again. It was lucky for the innkeeper that online reviews weren't a thing in this world. Danny's would've been scathing.

Judging by the shadows outside, he'd slept until around ten, crazy late for him. He'd probably be sleeping on the side of the road tonight. Though to be fair, he'd pretty much decided to sleep by the side of the road anyway. Even if he made it to a town, he was too broke to afford an inn every night.

Keeping to the edge of the road to avoid the many wagons clattering along the cobblestones, Danny made his way toward the north gate. The city seemed calm, which was both a good thing and rather odd, all things considered. The royal family must be doing a good job keeping the state of the kingdom a secret. Danny had heard no rumors during his time in the common room last night. It was mostly just people getting drunk and singing off-key. The scene reminded him of karaoke with the guys back home.

A couple blocks from the gate, Danny sensed a weak source of corruption approaching. He opened himself fully to the ether and soon located it. Some sort of flying demon headed right for the city. A quick glance around confirmed no was nearby.

One weak demon didn't seem like much of a threat, but just to be a good sport before he left, Danny summoned holy energy into his right hand and launched a spear of white light into the sky.

The demon was vaporized twenty yards from the wall.

He smiled to himself and got moving again. Maybe it was pointless, but hopefully he'd managed to keep some unlucky sap from getting killed. If so, it was well worth his time. It wasn't like the spell had cost him more than a negligible amount of energy.

Danny popped the last of his sandwich in his mouth and strode on. At the gate, the guards on duty raised their hands. One of them stepped forward. His red-and-gold uniform looked freshly pressed and if he was a day over twenty Danny would be shocked.

"Is there a problem, sir?" Danny asked.

"No, not a problem exactly," the young man said. "We have orders from the castle to warn anyone preparing to leave the city that monster activity in the countryside is elevated and any nonessential travel should be undertaken only at the most extreme need. It's my firm recommendation that you remain in the city for the time being."

"The warning is much appreciated, sir," Danny said. "However I have pressing business elsewhere, so I fear I can't heed it. If you'd raise the gate, I'd be much obliged."

The guard shrugged and motioned to the others. Soon the gate was clanking up.

"If you're killed, don't blame me."

Danny grinned. "If I'm killed, I won't be blaming anyone for anything ever again. Oh, I almost forgot to let you know, I met a wizard on my way here. He warned me that he sensed a demon not long ago and destroyed it as it approached the walls. I don't know if there are many more in the area, but I wanted to make sure you were aware. Good luck."

So saying Danny ducked under the still-rising portcullis and headed north. If anyone noticed his spell and came looking, the guards would mention the wizard he made up. It was likely a pointless coverup, but better safe than sorry.

Now to make some time. He had a long walk ahead of him and doubtless many dangers to face.

Richard strolled along the battlements near North Gate, his sullen-looking son following along with poorly disguised ill humor. It was a beautiful summer day, and while getting fresh air wasn't the point of the inspection, it was a nice side benefit. Richard spent far too much time inside reading depressing messages. He needed to know what was going on in the kingdom, but it was terribly frustrating to know what was happening and yet be largely powerless to do anything to fix the problems. It was one of the worst things about being a king.

Behind the royal duo, his bodyguards were keeping a discreet distance, though never so far away that they couldn't step in at a moment's notice. The six regular knights were led by an arcane knight. Keeping a magic user out of the field during the current emergency felt wrong, but with Lyra investigating Demon King Castle and the hero dead, someone capable of using magic needed to be in the castle on the off chance more demon assassins showed up.

The wall guard he was approaching came to attention and touched his right fist to his left shoulder in a crisp salute. Richard offered a smile and nod in return. He took comfort in their loyalty. Morale seemed good as well. No doubt it was the lack of fighting near Villipan City.

When they'd moved on Florian asked, "Are we going to walk all the way around the wall?"

"Yes, that's the whole point of the inspection. Do you have something more pressing to do?"

"More pressing? No. More interesting? Almost certainly. In fact, anything would be more interesting. This is a job for some officer, not the ruler and future ruler of the kingdom."

"That's where you're wrong, son." Richard glanced at his sour-faced second child, praying Adonael wouldn't let anything happen to him until the boy had matured a bit more. "Letting the men see you and showing you're interested in them helps build a bond between ruler and subject. These men may one day be called upon to lay down their lives for you. It would hurt nothing if they saw you as a real person and not a faceless name."

As they approached the next man in line, Richard frowned. The guard was staring out over the wall toward something in the northern sky. Shading his eyes, Richard could barely make out a black shape headed this way. Was it a raven? He couldn't tell for sure.

"What do you see, soldier?" Richard asked.

The guard about jumped out of his skin when the king spoke. "Begging your pardon, Majesty, but I can't tell yet what it is. All I know for sure is that it's headed this way. The officers told everyone to be extra alert, but I hate to raise a fuss if it's only a crow."

"That's no crow!" Alard, the arcane knight in charge of his security, had his sword drawn and was running toward Richard. "It's a demon. I can sense its corruption from here. Get behind me, Majesty."

Before Richard could move, a line of white light streaked up and reduced the demon to a puff of black smoke.

"What the hell was that?" Florian asked.

"A holy lance," Alard said. "A powerful one. Looks like someone on the ground spotted the demon as well. Perhaps an adventuring wizard or one of Adonael's priests—a couple have returned from the field. In any case, it might be best to cut the inspection short. I can't sense any more corruption at the moment, but another demon might be lurking beyond my range."

Richard hesitated, weighing the risk of looking weak against the danger of a second demon. In the end there was really no choice. "Very well, let's return to the castle. And send someone to find out who cast that spell. Whoever it was is clearly no friend to the demons. I'd like to offer them a proper thank-you."

Alard pointed at one of the knights. "You heard His

Majesty. See what you can find out. The rest of you, fall in to defensive positions."

The chosen guard trotted off while Richard and the rest headed directly back to the castle. His pleasant stroll had come to an abrupt end. Pity, but when there were demons flying around, what could you do?

CHAPTER 7

The walls of Rosenbar appeared in the distance. The journey had gone more smoothly than Danny feared it might. Since he was traveling alone, he had no qualms about using the ethersword. It was every bit as effective as Merrok had claimed and Danny even killed one demon by smashing it in the face with the mithril hilt. Four encounters with low-level demons and ogres had barely made him sweat. A part of him had wondered if dying and being resurrected would mess with his inherited abilities, but so far, both his magic and fighting skills appeared to be in working order. Though until he fought something really strong he wouldn't be totally confident.

He knew there had to be a finite number of monsters in the Five Kingdoms, but if a lone traveler had run into four groups he shuddered to think how many might be out there. On the plus side, Danny wouldn't be short of work in his new career as an adventurer. Assuming, of course, that he could find the guild and join without issue. Not that he could think of an issue. As with any other guild, he'd have to follow the rules and obey his superiors. Just like the Marines.

Then again, that was pure speculation on Danny's part, and pointless speculation to boot. He was only delaying the moment of truth, letting his nerves get the best of him. No royal authority backed him now. The hero was dead and Danny was a nobody. A broke nobody.

Enough fooling around. He got moving again, heading straight for the closed southern gate. Ten guards were on duty, all of them armed with spears and dressed in mail. Neither any wagon nor a bit of foot traffic waited to enter. Not ideal from Danny's point of view since it would make him stand out. But, as with all his other concerns, this one was outside his control.

As he got closer, eight of the guards formed a semicircle with their spears pointed at him while two others stayed behind them. One of them glowed in the ether. A wizard or priest then. That was good. He could enchant the guards' weapons so they would have a chance against a demon. The other fellow was probably the unit commander.

"Halt!" said the one he assumed was in charge. "What's your business in Rosenbar?"

"I'm hoping to find work at the Adventurers' Guild."

The wizard nodded and said, "I sense no corruption and there's no aura that indicates an illusory disguise. He's human and he didn't lie."

The spearmen let out an audible gasp of relief.

"Are things that bad around here?" Danny asked.

"They're bad enough," the commander said. "You're the first person to arrive in several weeks. How did you manage that anyway?"

He sounded suspicious. Since the wizard could detect

lies, Danny would have to be careful how he answered. "I'm good at stealth magic. Watch."

He activated his stealth field. Judging from their expressions, the invisibility had them impressed.

"It's hard to attack something you can't see." He reappeared and flashed a grin.

"With magic like that," the commander said. "You'll have no trouble finding work. In you get."

The portcullis clanked up about four feet, forcing Danny to duck under it. As soon as he was clear it slammed back down. He couldn't fault the guards for their precautions. If anything, he felt like Rosenbar was taking security more seriously than the capital. Maybe the demon Danny fried would help the people in charge focus.

He shook his head. Capital security wasn't his concern. Right now, he needed to find the Adventurers' Guild. In fact, he should've asked the guards where to find it, but they were so tense he hadn't wanted to hang around. He glanced around the open area beyond the gate. There were no people outside. The road directly ahead led to the central district and the mayor's castle. Danny didn't want to go that way. He doubted anyone would recognize him with his bald head and beard, but why risk it?

He snapped his fingers. When he arrived with Robi and Trevor they'd gone right. At least he was pretty sure that's what he remembered. He had half a day's worth of light left; surely he could find someone to give him directions before dark.

With a little shrug, Danny set out. The streets and buildings looked very much like the capital. Most were a couple stories tall and made of stone with tile roofs. A block from the gate he found an open store. "Dry goods" it said above the door, along with a picture of what Danny guessed was supposed to be a burlap sack. Interesting symbol for dry goods.

A little copper bell jingled when he pushed the door open. Inside, half the shelves were empty. He took a quick walk around and found some tools—picks, hoes, and axes mostly. Barrels with nails of various sizes lined one shelf. The only food he found were dried beans and bags of barley. Slim pickings, no doubt.

When he made his way to the checkout counter he found a weathered old man waiting. Deep-set eyes looked Danny up and down then he gave a little shake of his head. "You don't want any dry goods, do you, son?"

"No, sir, I'm afraid I don't. The thing is, I just arrived in Rosenbar and I'm trying to find the Adventurers' Guild. Would you be kind enough to point me in the right direction?"

"Figured you were an adventurer. You've got the look."

Danny smiled. "What look is that, sir?"

"Broke and hungry."

Danny laughed. "You're not wrong. I'm down to my last small silver coin and three strips of jerky. If the guild charges more than that to join, I'm doomed."

The shopkeeper smiled. "Never fear, son, there's no fee to join the guild. Given the survival rate of new adventurers they can't afford to turn anyone away. Go out the door, take a right. Straight for three blocks, then a left. One block after that and it'll be on your right. Big brick building with a sign featuring a crossed sword and wand. Can't miss it."

He nodded. "Thanks. If I ever need dry goods, I'll be back."

The old man shook his head and waved him off. Danny

waved back and ducked out the door. He had to admit, the odds of him needing dry goods did seem pretty low. But then again who could say when a fifty-pound bag of dried beans might come in handy? If you dropped it on someone's head it would do a fair bit of damage.

Following the directions he'd been provided, Danny soon found himself standing across the street from a gray brick building. There was no shouting or rowdiness at the moment. Maybe they were all out on quests.

Taking a deep breath, Danny pushed the door open. Inside was what looked like a reception area. There were scattered tables and chairs and along the back ran a counter with two people, a man and a woman, both dressed in tan tunics, standing behind it. Most of the tables were occupied, largely by glowering men and glaring women, all of them armed to the teeth. Every eye shifted to Danny and not a one looked friendly.

It seemed business was not good for the Rosenbar Adventurers' Guild. That came as a surprise given all the monsters running around. Oh well, hopefully that meant more work for Danny.

He made it halfway across the room before a six-and-a-half-foot-tall bruiser pushed away from his table and moved to block the path. It was such a cliché that Danny had to restrain a laugh. This must be the "asshole testing the new guy's resolve" part of signing up.

Best to try and move things along peacefully. "Excuse me."

The big guy didn't so much as flinch.

Okay, so much for peacefully. "I said, excuse me. That means get the fuck out of the way in polite society."

The big guy shook his head. "Can't do that. It's awful

dangerous beyond the wall. New adventurers are dying faster than they can join. A kid like you wouldn't last five minutes outside. Hell, most of us won't go out on jobs anymore. Why don't you go on home and find something safer to do?"

Huh, maybe he wasn't so bad after all. "I appreciate the warning. However, I'm determined to join. If I get torn apart by demons that'll be on me. Okay?"

That brought another shake of the head. "I'm already an elite adventurer. If you can make me move, then you can join. If you can't, then you have to leave."

Now Danny was getting annoyed. "Look, whoever you are, I don't need your permission. I'm willing to give you the benefit of the doubt and assume your intentions are good. However, good intentions or not, this is none of your business."

Arms as big as Danny's legs crossed over his massive chest. A silent glare was the only response he got.

Fine, whatever. Danny activated his stealth field, becoming invisible and silent. He slipped around the now-befuddled-looking warrior and made his way to the counter. When he stood in front of the woman he let the spell fade.

She flinched and let out a little yelp. Danny put her age at about ten years his senior. Like everyone in this country, she had long blond hair and bright blue eyes. She also had a nice figure, but nothing to compare to Claudette.

"Sorry, you startled me," the secretary said. "I couldn't help overhearing your conversation with Bruno. You want to join?"

"Yes, ma'am."

"Hey!" Bruno stomped back to the counter to loom over

Danny. "I said you had to make me move, not use some trick to sneak around."

"I did make you move," Danny said. "You were over there, now you're over here. I win."

The secretary let out a little giggle, drawing a glower from Bruno. "Do you want this kid to get killed, Emily? You know that's what'll happen if you let him sign up. It's hell out there right now."

Emily sighed. "Your heart's in the right place, Bruno, but it's not for me or you to decide what a person can do with their lives. It's his choice, not ours."

Bruno looked so pained that Danny felt a little bad for him. "I'm stronger than I look, I promise. And I can use magic. Please don't worry about me."

Massive shoulders slumped. "Fine. I tried."

Bruno trudged back to his seat and dropped into a remarkably sturdy chair.

"I apologize for that," Emily said. "He's scared off three new recruits already this month. You're the first to make it past him since the demon king was slain."

"Why does your guild master or whoever runs this place put up with that sort of thing?"

"Actually, the guild master encourages him. If a new recruit can't make it past Bruno, they'd have no hope out in the field, not now anyway. We do need new members, but not dead ones." Emily reached under the counter and pulled out a pot of ink, a quill, and a questionnaire. "Anyway, let's get started. Are you good to fill this out by yourself?"

"I'm not that young."

"Ah, no, it's just that a lot of our recruits come from the country and can't read or write so I have to fill out the form for them."

Danny knew in theory that literacy wasn't a common thing on this world, but the idea that someone couldn't fill out a simple form was so foreign to him that he hadn't really understood what it meant.

"I'll be fine, ma'am. Thank you." He spun the questionnaire around for a closer look.

"Please, call me Emily. When you say ma'am, it makes me feel old."

"My apologies, Emily." Danny smiled. "I was only trying to be respectful."

"Your mother raised you well. Wave at me when you're finished." She wandered down to chat with her male counterpart.

Okay, let's see. Name, that was easy. He put in his new identity of Ronin. Age, sixteen. Job, that was tricky. He assumed it meant warrior or wizard or something. Hero struck him as a poor thing to put down so he went with arcane knight. There were questions about his general health, his hometown, and his family. Danny made up answers based on names he'd seen on a map. He doubted they had time to check up on him in any case. This was likely just a way to contact his next of kin after he got killed.

When he finished, Danny waved at Emily. She hurried over and took the questionnaire back. After a cursory glance which confirmed his theory that it didn't matter, she said, "Looks good. I think you're the youngest arcane knight we've ever had. Since I've already seen your magic, I'm confident you're not lying. That's always a plus."

"Why would someone lie about their skills? As soon as they were out in the field it would be revealed, right?"

Emily shrugged. "Why do people do a lot of the things they do? I wish I knew. Now there's the matter of your ranking match. The guild master has to oversee it himself. He's with a client right now, but as soon as he finishes up, I'm sure he'll be eager to get started."

Since no one was waiting in line behind him Danny asked, "What's a ranking match?"

"Oh, right, I guess I should explain about guild ranks. It's pretty simple. New arrivals are ranked either beginner or journeyman. The results of your match will determine that. Once you successfully complete ten jobs, you'll be upgraded to elite."

"What does that get you?" Danny asked.

"Respect mostly. It shows you're reliable. A lot of nobles won't hire an adventurer lower than elite." Emily looked around as if afraid someone might be listening. "I'll let you in on a secret. Many adventurers are really looking for a permanent position as a noble's bodyguard. Way easier job with better pay. Building up your reputation is the best way to attract attention."

"Good to know, but life as a bodyguard doesn't interest me. What are the other ranks?"

"After elite comes alpha elite or A rank. You have to complete one hundred jobs for that promotion. Almost no one does since they tend to end up dead or hired by a noble before then. Finally there's super elite or S rank. For that you need two hundred and fifty complete jobs and at least three guild masters who will say you're the strongest adventurer in their guild. It's very rare. In fact, I don't think there's an S-rank adventurer in the Five Kingdoms at the moment."

"There was in the past?" Danny asked.

"I believe so, though it was over five hundred years ago. She wasn't from the Five Kingdoms, only visiting during a world tour. Of course it could also be made up. I read about it in the guild history books."

A door slammed deeper in the building, cutting off their conversation. A moment later two men emerged from a passage to Danny's right. One of the men had gray hair, a lean build, and wore a dark tunic and trousers. The second man was well known to Danny. Trevor's bald head and chubby build were unmistakable. The merchant did not look well pleased.

"Look," the older man said. "You can keep your request up, but I don't think anyone's going to take it. Guard work is too dangerous right now. You should wait until the army finishes thinning out the monsters."

"At the rate the early harvest is rotting," Trevor said, "by the time the army is finished, nothing will remain to collect. Robi and his team are willing, but there aren't enough of them. If you don't take the risk now, we'll be starving by midwinter."

"You don't know that. The fall harvest might make up for it. And maybe dead in six months sounds a lot better than definitely dead right now." The older man shrugged. "I can't order anyone to take your job. That's not how the guild works."

"I know, I know." Trevor blew out a long, frustrated sigh. "I appreciate you listening to me."

"Anytime, old friend, anytime."

Once the door closed behind Trevor, Emily said, "Sir, we have a new recruit that needs to be tested."

The old man—the guild master, Danny assumed—shot him a stern but not unkind look before joining them at the counter. "Made it past Bruno, did you? Must be made of sterner stuff than our last few potential recruits. The test is a two-minute sparring match with one of our journeymen adventurers. Are you okay with that?"

Danny nodded. "If that's what needs to happen, then sure. Where is the match held, out back?"

"No room in the city for an outdoor training area, unfortunately," the guild master said. "We set one up in the basement. Don't worry, we brought in plenty of sand so any impacts won't hurt too bad. Plus, I'm a priest of Branik. I can heal most any injury."

"That's reassuring."

The guild master shot him a conflicted look. "You're sure you want to do this? No shame in changing your mind."

He must have misunderstood Danny's relief. He wasn't worried about getting hurt; he was worried he might do someone permanent damage. "I'm good to go. What are the rules?"

"I'll go over them right before the match just to be sure you both understand." The guild master shifted to look out over the crowd. "I need a journeyman for a ranking match. Anyone up for it?"

Every hand in the room went up. That was vaguely insulting.

The guild master glared at Bruno. "Journeymen only. You know the rules."

Four hands, including Bruno's, went down. Did they really have so few experienced adventurers here?

"Floyd." The guild master pointed at a young man maybe two years older than Danny's host body. "You're up."

Floyd stood and grinned. His blond hair was cropped close and he had a wiry build, at least judging by the arms his sleeveless tan tunic left exposed.

"He should be a good match for you," the guild master said. "Floyd just ranked up to journeyman six months ago."

Danny nodded. He saw no aura of magic around Floyd. If he had any magical ability he hid it well. More likely he was a pure fighter. Though he would never underestimate an opponent, Danny was confident a straight fighter had little chance against him.

"Who's ready for a match?" the guild master shouted.

A roar went up from the gathered adventurers. It looked like Danny was going to have an audience.

CHAPTER 8

Lyra stood outside the gates of Demon King Castle and stared up at the black walls. She'd never visited the castle by herself. There had never been any reason to. She came with the hero and his companions, they fought, the demon king was defeated, and they left. But this time something had gone wrong. If Adonael was right, and Lyra was not going to doubt the word of an archangel, then somehow the demon king had escaped. King Richard believed she'd find some clue to the woman's location in the castle.

That seemed unlikely to Lyra. Why would you leave a clue to your plans in the one place you could be almost certain your enemies might look? Everything she'd seen led her to believe this demon king was smart, maybe the smartest one they'd ever faced. She vastly preferred the strong, stupid sort of enemy.

Pity she didn't get a say in what sort of champion the demon lords sent their way.

Shaking off her thoughts, she strode right up to the main

castle gate. The heavy black double doors were closed tight. There were no pulls on the outside. She focused on the ether but had to quickly look away. It was so corrupted that any extended use would damage her eyes. There was one way around that.

She opened her pocket dimension and pulled out the hero's sword. The oppressive weight of the corruption immediately lifted. It had surprised her when Daniel didn't ask for the sword and armor. They were powerful tools. He did have the ethersword, which was nearly as good. Perhaps the hero's gear left a bad taste in his mouth.

Drawing ether through the sword, she tried again.

And failed again. There was simply nothing to see. No hidden latch or rune would open the gate. It was sealed until the demon king returned, just as she feared. The only option remaining was to force it open.

Strengthening her body with purified ether, she drew back and swung the hero's sword with all her might. The blade cut a two-inch-deep groove in the black wood. So it could be damaged. That was something.

Ten minutes of hacking finally opened a jagged passage just big enough for her to slip inside. Ten feet beyond the opening, the hall was pitch black. She conjured a white light and focused it around the sword's blade. The hall looked exactly like she remembered.

Lyra walked slowly deeper into the castle, every sense alert for potential danger. As far as she could tell, nothing hid in the dark. No demons, no blackguards, no undead, no nothing. Her footsteps echoed through the empty halls. She even stomped a couple times in the hope of drawing the attention of something, anything, to break the silence.

And maybe she succeeded. Directly ahead of her a crimson flame burst to life.

Lyra raised her sword, ready for a fight.

But she didn't get one. The flame just hung there, bobbing like a duck on a pond. With no better options, she moved closer, careful to keep the sword between her and the flame.

When she was three feet away another flame, a twin to the first, appeared further up the hall. Didn't take a genius to figure out she was being led somewhere. Whether she wanted to go there was another matter, but since this was the first interesting thing she'd seen since arriving, Lyra figured she might as well follow it and see what happened.

The flames led her away from the central chamber where the final battle with the demon king always took place. Instead they went down a curved hall she was fairly sure hadn't existed before. It spiraled slowly downward before ending in an archway which led to a large, open chamber. The only thing of note in the room was the huge crimson flame burning in the center. It reached from the floor all the way to the ceiling.

Lyra hesitated a moment then shrugged and strode into the room. She stopped ten feet from the pillar of flame.

"How perfect that you should come to visit me," a rich, sultry female voice said. "I've always had a soft spot for women who murder unsuspecting men. You would be far happier serving me than pretending to care about humans."

Lyra grimaced to hear her betrayal praised. There was only one being she could think of who had a voice like that who would take such an attitude. "Ardent Lilly. Why have you guided me here?"

"So we could chat, dear child. Nowhere in Valindor is

more closely connected to my hell at the moment. You're practically standing on my doorstep. Since Adonael has already spilled the news that my champion survived, I thought, why not have a visit? Who knows, you might trick me into revealing some important secret."

Lyra seriously doubted that, but it wouldn't hurt to listen. "How did she escape?"

"Magic. Much like your latest hero, my champion made prior arrangements should she fall in battle. You've become rather predictable with your trick of murdering the hero after he wins the final battle. Rather ungrateful of you, killing your savior so you don't have to pay for his retirement. That's the sort of thing I might do. Deceiving you into doing our job for us was amusing. Of course, even I didn't predict the hero finding a way to save himself. That was less amusing. Still, you did ensure that he would never lift a finger to help you again, so that's a partial win."

"I don't need to be reminded of my failings."

"But it's so much fun. You elf-bloods are so arrogant and sure of the wisdom your long lives bring. It makes your failures so much more enjoyable."

Lyra bit back a snarling reply. She refused to let this creature get the best of her. "Where is the demon king now?"

"She's in many places, all far from here. She will gather her power and in her own time return to wipe this miserable, heroless country off the map before smashing the cathedral and claiming this world for me. Just thinking about Null's reaction when I win sends a shiver up my spine." A ripple ran through the flames like it was actually shivering.

"You didn't answer my question."

Mocking laughter filled the chamber. "What did you think I was going to say? Did you imagine I'd provide you an address? She's right here, go try and kill her if you dare. Perish the thought. If you wish to try and hunt her down, go ahead. This is a big world, but you might stumble over her. You'll find no clues here. My champion is far too clever to make such a simple mistake. Personally, I'd recommend going home and enjoying whatever time you have left with your granddaughters before the end."

"You're wasting my time."

"You already wasted your time by coming here. I know you have to obey your master like an obedient dog, but you had to know it was a waste of time. You would've accomplished more fighting monsters in the countryside. Not a lot more, but still."

Lyra turned to leave. She'd had all she could take of this creature.

"Leaving already? I so seldom get company." Mocking laughter followed Lyra all the way to the top of the spiral path.

She debated just leaving now, but figured it wouldn't hurt to search the rest of the castle. Ardent Lilly was a liar, so maybe she'd find something useful. Lyra swallowed a sigh. Bad enough she had to listen to a demon lord; now she was lying to herself.

CHAPTER 9

The basement of the Rosenbar Adventurers' Guild was a single large space broken up only by stone pillars that supported the weight of the building. Racks of weapons ran along the walls and targets of various sorts had been set up.

The middle third of the room held a circle filled with sand. It looked a bit like the floor of a gladiatorial arena, or at least the ones Danny had seen in movies. The guild master walked into the center of the circle and beckoned Danny and Floyd to join him. The rest of the adventurers formed a second circle around the sand. They were all grinning, seeming eager for the match. Given the dearth of entertainment options in Villipan, that didn't surprise Danny in the least.

"Okay, listen up," the guild master said. "It's time for a ranking match. The rules are simple. If Ronin, our new member, can stay in the circle for two minutes, knock Floyd out of the circle or render him unconscious, he'll receive the rank of journeyman. Otherwise, he'll start out as a beginner.

As for the fight, it's blunt weapons only, no armor. If you can use magic, go ahead, but no lethal spells, obviously. Questions?"

Danny shook his head. The rules were simple enough, though the lack of protective gear seemed unwise, but whatever. He didn't plan on getting hit in any case. Floyd grinned at him. It wasn't the nasty sort of grin that said he was looking forward to beating Danny to a pulp, but rather a friendly one as if to say no hard feelings. That's how Danny read it anyway.

"What are your weapons?" the guild master asked.

"Arming sword and shield for me," Floyd said.

One of the other adventurers trotted over to the correct rack and returned with a two-and-a-half-foot-long wooden sword with a grip just big enough for one hand as well as a round shield about three feet across.

Danny planned to use magic so he said, "A longsword will be fine for me. Oh, I suppose I should take these off."

While someone went to get his practice weapon, Danny removed the baldric which held his sword and dagger and passed them to the guild master. He accepted a heavy wooden sword about three feet long with a two-handed grip. The balance was decent and the heft reasonable. No katanas hung on the wall. The weapon seemed pretty rare. In fact, the hero's sword was the only one Danny had seen.

"Remember the rules." The guild master took a small hourglass out of his pocket. As he spoke, Danny silently activated physical enhancements that would make his bones harder than steel and his skin impenetrable. Not that he had any intention of getting hit. "And when I tell you to stop, you stop. Ready?"

Danny nodded and a moment later Floyd said, "Ready."

The guild master flipped the hourglass over. "Begin!"

Before Floyd could take a step, Danny sent four arcs of lightning lancing out, one for each of his opponent's limbs. He was careful not to let any of the electricity travel to Floyd's vital organs. Instead Danny caused his limbs to spasm. Two seconds into the match, sparks were popping off of Floyd's skin as he lay twitching on the sand.

Danny glanced at the guild master. "Is that good enough?"

Some of the watching adventurers grumbled amongst themselves. They had clearly been expecting a more entertaining show. He could've given them one, but wasn't in the mood to fool around at the moment.

"Um, yeah. That was a bit quicker than I figured the match was going to be, but you certainly won it fair and square." Once the guild master made it official, Danny ended the lightning spell. "When you went for a longsword I figured you were going to use the reach advantage to hold Floyd off until you ran out of time. The lightning was a total shock, pun intended."

Danny leaned on the wooden sword. "That's what I meant for you all to think. No one expects the guy with the big sword to be a wizard. My teacher called it manipulating expectations."

"Clever. What was his name?"

"Sir Parker," Danny said, giving the name of his drill sergeant from basic. "Toughest man I ever knew."

"I'm not familiar with him," the guild master said.

"I'm not surprised," Danny said. "He was a quiet man who kept to himself. I got the impression that he saw some things when he was younger that left mental scars. I respected his privacy. So what happens now?"

"Now we'll go upstairs, get you an identification badge,

and make a quick run-through of the guild rules. Oh, one moment." The guild master went and passed a glowing hand over Floyd. "There, all better."

Floyd let out a groan and pushed himself to his feet. "You sure got me. I figured that invisibility trick was the only one you knew."

Danny grinned. "Making assumptions isn't the healthiest idea. Sorry you didn't get a chance to show off your moves."

"Eh, no problem. Give me your sword and I'll put it back. Least I can do after the whooping you gave me. With skills like yours, you'll be elite in no time."

Bruno snorted. "Skills or not, if you go outside the walls, you'll be dead. Don't forget that. Rank's no use to a corpse."

On that grim note, the gathering broke up. Danny took his baldric back and buckled it on.

"Let's go upstairs," the guild master said. "Emily can make your badge while we talk in my office. I'll also give you the two-copper tour."

"Sure, thanks." Danny followed his new boss back up the steps. On the way to the reception counter they paused in front of what looked like a cork board covered with half a dozen sheets of paper. "What's this?"

"The job board. This is where people post jobs for adventurers. Pretty sparse at the moment. Our work generally takes us outside the city and right now no one's moving. Most of our patrons are merchants and nobles. What's bad for them is bad for us."

"Demons are bad for pretty much everyone," Danny said.

"Can't argue with that. I'll show you what goes into a job post. It's pretty simple." The guild master pulled a paper down and held it out to show Danny. "At the top is the job name, bodyguard in this case. Next is the minimum rank, journeyman. Followed by a description. This lady is meeting a gentleman for their first date and wants someone to keep a quiet eye on them to make sure he doesn't try anything inappropriate."

"If she's worried her date is going to assault her," Danny said. "Maybe she should find a different guy."

The guild master shrugged. "True, but if she did that, we'd have one less job. This would actually be a good one for you. That invisibility spell of yours makes you perfect for this sort of thing. Anyway, below the description is the reward, in this case five small silver coins. At the end of the job, the client signs on the line at the bottom. You return with the contract and we pay you, minus our ten percent fee of course."

"I was just going to ask how you paid your bills. Seems simple enough. What if more than one person wants a job?"

"First come, first served. If you see a job that interests you and is appropriate for your rank, grab it. Come on."

They went to the counter next and Emily smiled at him. "Quick match. What sort of badge should I make?"

"Journeyman," the guild master said. "We'll be in my office going over the rules. Just bring it up when you're done."

"Yes, sir," Emily said. "And congratulations, Ronin. Getting started as a journeyman is amazing."

"Thanks." Danny felt a bit sheepish at the praise. As the hero, or former hero, a match against a normal man was never going to be a challenge for him.

He followed the guild master down a short hall to his office. There was a desk, some chairs, and a bookcase. The only remarkable thing about it was a huge iron safe that covered half of one wall. The safe glowed bright in Danny's magical vision.

"Caught your attention, did it?" The guild master sat behind his desk. "That's the guild's treasury. We also hold some of the members' savings as well. The safe is heavily warded against all forms of unauthorized opening. If you ever have excess funds, we'd be happy to store them for you."

Danny figured he'd keep his money and gear in his personal storage. "That's generous of you, thanks."

"It's one of the perks of membership. Have a seat." When Danny had settled down in the chair across from him the guild master said, "We don't have many rules. As long as you follow them and don't cause trouble you'll fit right in."

"I'll do my best. Before you get started can I ask a question?"

"Of course."

"Why 'Adventurers' Guild'? We're basically mercenaries. Wouldn't that be a better name?"

"It might be, but there's already a mercenaries' guild and they wouldn't take kindly to us using their name. Plus, our members do plenty of noncombat-related tasks: hunting, collecting rare herbs, that sort of thing."

"What do the mercenaries do?"

"Pure combat. And they have different membership requirements. To join as a captain, you need to have a minimum of fifty men at arms under your command. They handle contracts like we do and like us their organization is transnational. You can find mercenary guilds all over the world."

"Interesting. Sorry to sidetrack the conversation. You were going to tell me the rules."

"Right." The guild master pulled a scroll out of his desk drawer and handed it to Danny. "This is your copy. Basically, the guild acts as an intermediary with clients. We hold your payments until the job is complete and we certify that you have the necessary skills to complete the job by giving you a rank. You know you're going to get paid and the client knows you're not some random person talking big. That said, we take no responsibility for your success or failure. Stuff happens in the field and there are no guarantees.

"Fights between members are forbidden except in training. You can form temporary partnerships for big jobs and we'll make sure the money is split correctly. And that's about it. Oh, Timothy can sell you supplies should you need any. Nothing magical, but common weapons, rations, and other ordinary stuff is no problem."

"Who's Timothy?" Danny asked.

"The gentleman at the counter. Emily handles jobs and registration and Timothy handles supplies and basically any other odd job that pops up. At some point, I would recommend you join the wizards' guild in Villipan City as well. You're obviously skilled in magic and they have a well-stocked library that would no doubt do a lot to increase your knowledge."

"I appreciate the advice. Is it a big deal if I do magic without being a member?"

"You can't open up a magic shop unless you're a member, but they wouldn't try and tell you how to use your personal magic."

Danny had no interest in opening a magic shop and he also had no intention of returning to Villipan City. "Got it. Anything else?"

Someone knocked on the door before the guild master had a chance to answer. "Come in."

Emily opened the door and came over to the desk. She

had on a knee-length dark skirt along with her tan tunic. He hadn't noticed it when she was behind the counter.

"I've got the badge ready." She held it out to Danny.

He took it. The badge was round and made of copper with the guild symbol stamped into one side. On the other was his new name and the word "journeyman." That was it, nothing fancy and nothing magic.

"Thank you."

"Make sure you don't lose it. Your badge can get you into a lot of cities that might otherwise give you a hassle," the guild master said.

"Why would any city give me a problem about entering?"

"Some places are more xenophobic than others. I doubt you'll have any trouble in the Five Kingdoms, but if you travel beyond them, the rules can change. Do you plan to travel beyond the Five Kingdoms?"

"Yes, my eventual goal is to see the world. I found an old map in one of my teacher's books and couldn't get over how big the continent was. Though I don't know if it's possible to explore the whole thing in one lifetime, I mean to try."

"A worthy goal," the guild master said.

"Sounds romantic," Emily added.

"At the very least it's better than wanting to become some noble's hired muscle," the guild master said. "Do you want a piece of advice?"

"Please. I'm very new to the adventuring lifestyle. Any and all advice is welcome."

"Stick around here until you reach elite status. Having that on your badge will open a lot of doors. Plus, I can't imagine how difficult it would be to pass through Fell Forest at the moment."

"That's not a bad plan," Danny said. "Also, I'm broke.

Saving up some traveling money wouldn't be the worst idea. Is there anything else?"

"No, I think that's it." The guild master stood and held out his hand. "Feel free to ask for advice anytime. That's what I'm here for."

Danny shook his hand. "Thanks. I didn't catch your name."

"Sorry about that. Everyone just calls me Guild Master here, so I often forget to introduce myself. Name's Duret. Feel free to call me either. Will you be taking that job guarding the lady?"

"No, I've got an idea I think might help your friend the merchant."

Duret frowned. "That's a damn risky option for your first job. You sure?"

"I heard what he said about starving this winter. Can't say that overly appeals to me. Besides, I assume that the more dangerous the job, the better it pays."

"You're right about that," Duret said. "But remember what Bruno told you about rank? Gold is of equally little use to the dead."

Danny nodded, left the office, and made his way back to the job board. It didn't take long to find Trevor's post. Interestingly, he'd left six copies of the job. That must be how many people he wanted. Danny took one and left the rest.

Minimum rank was journeyman, no problem there. The job title was caravan guard, as expected. The details were simple as well. Protect the wagons as they traveled between farms collecting food then back to Rosenbar. The pay was five small gold pieces upon their safe return to the city. One coin would be subtracted for every wagon lost. So if they made it back alive, the minimum pay was one gold coin.

Pretty generous. The final bit of information was the location of Trevor's warehouse.

Danny folded up the contract and slipped it into his pocket. He couldn't say he was excited about his first job as an adventurer, but the money would be nice and stocking up on food wouldn't hurt either. If he was lucky, maybe Trevor would let him sleep in the warehouse. Given his new appearance there was no way they'd recognize him, especially since everyone likely knew the hero was dead.

CHAPTER 10

I t wasn't a long walk from the guild to Trevor's warehouse and Danny made the trip in about fifteen minutes. The building was huge and built from stone with a set of double doors in the front big enough to let the wagons go in and out with room to spare. To the left of the main doors was a smaller one for people. The building glowed in the ether and Danny assumed that was the preservation magic Trevor had mentioned when Danny and his companions rescued him.

The walk here had given him some time to think over his approach. In the end, Danny figured direct was the best way to go. It sounded like Trevor was pretty desperate. Any reasonable plan was likely to get a positive response.

He blew out a final breath and strode up to the small door. A couple firm raps should get someone's attention. Sure enough, less than a minute later the door opened and Danny found himself face to face with Robi. The leader of the first group of adventurers Danny had ever met looked a bit worse for wear. His eyes were shadowed and a scruffy beard covered his face.

"Sorry," Robi said. "We don't sell direct to the public here. You'll have to go to one of the regular merchants."

"I'm not here to shop." Danny pulled out his badge and showed it to Robi. "I'm here to join the team."

Robi brightened. "Where's the rest of your group?"

"I'm solo."

"Oh." His shoulders slumped again. "We appreciate the help, but even one more person isn't going to be enough."

"The right person might be," Danny said. "I'm good at stealth magic. If I scout ahead for you, we could avoid, or at least not get ambushed by, any enemies we might encounter. I can also enchant your weapons with holy magic. If the situation is as dire as your employer made it sound at the guild today, I figured it might be worth a shot."

"Stealth and holy magic; you're a man of many talents. With that combination we might just be able to make it work. At the very least it's worth talking to Master Trevor. Name's Robi, I'm in charge of security."

"Ronin." They shook hands and Robi let him inside. Danny looked all around at the rows of empty shelves. The warehouse was less than a quarter filled with baskets of vegetables and hanging sides of meat. "Wow, it really is sparse in here. I was hoping Trevor had been exaggerating for effect. This can't be all the food in the city."

"No, thank Adonael." Robi started across the warehouse and Danny fell in beside him. "The Crown has a number of grain silos and there are smaller merchants with warehouses as well, though none as big as this and none that are enchanted to protect against spoilage. The fall harvest doesn't start for another couple months, so hopefully the demons will be cleaned up and we can make up for lost time."

"You don't sound optimistic," Danny said.

"No. The problem is the demons are destroying the crops, killing the livestock, and corrupting everything to make it unusable. At the rate they're going, nothing will remain to harvest when fall arrives. That's why we're so desperate to get what we can now."

"I'll do my best to help."

Robi clapped him on the shoulder. "Good to see some of my fellow adventurers have a spine. Speaking of, assuming Master Trevor says yes, I'll introduce you to the rest of the team. They're a good group—skilled, trustworthy, everything you could ask for in a party. We've been together for five years."

They reached a door in the rear wall, and Robi knocked. "Sir? We've got a new recruit."

The door opened and Trevor's rumpled, sweaty figure appeared in the entrance. "Just one?"

He sounded so disappointed.

"Yes, sir. This is Ronin and he's a wizard."

"Arcane knight, technically." Danny held out his hand and got a clammy shake. "I heard you speaking with the guild master and came over in the hope that I might be able to help."

"He's got a plan I think might do the trick," Robi said.

"Come in and tell me about it." Trevor moved aside to let them in. "I refuse to get my hopes up, but at this point I'm willing to consider anything remotely reasonable."

Trevor's office was pretty much a duplicate of Duret's at the guild, only with more papers on the desk and a smaller safe. They settled into the chairs and Danny repeated what he'd told Robi. When he finished he said, "I think it'll work, but ultimately the decision is yours."

Trevor's brow furrowed as he thought. It was a big risk and Danny didn't blame him for being hesitant. As far as Trevor knew, Danny was a brand-new adventurer. Staking a bunch of lives on someone like him was a big gamble.

"Show me this stealth spell of yours," Trevor said. "If Robi says it's good enough, we'll risk a run. If not, you're welcome to sign on, but until we get a few more people, we'll have to wait."

Danny stood. That was fair. A moment of concentration activated the spell. Danny slipped around the desk to stand behind Trevor. Both men were staring at the spot he'd occupied a moment earlier.

He waited a few seconds then released the spell. "What do you think?"

Trevor nearly leapt out of his chair.

Robi grinned. "I neither saw, heard, nor sensed anything. In fact, I've never encountered such an effective stealth spell. How long can you maintain it?"

"Activating it takes a bit of power, but maintaining it is easy. I can go for hours. I figure I'll head out first then you follow half an hour later. I'll rejoin you for the noon break, assuming I don't run into anything dangerous. Some food and an hour of rest and I'll be good to go until we stop to make camp."

"I think it'll work, sir," Robi said. "We can make a short run first, just a couple wagons, and if that goes okay, we can try something more ambitious."

Trevor nodded. He still looked nervous, but now determination had joined the mix. "Agreed. I'll make preparations and you'll leave in the morning."

"I'm going to introduce Ronin to the rest of the team."

"Good idea," Trevor said.

"One question if I may," Danny said.

"Go ahead," Trevor said.

"Can I sleep here tonight? I'm pretty much broke."

The two men stared at him for a moment then started laughing. When they caught their breath Robi said, "You can bunk with the team. We've got a sort of barracks attached to the warehouse. It's nothing fancy, but I think we can find you a cot and a bowl of stew."

"That would suit me very well," Danny said. "Thank you."

"If this plan of yours works," Trevor said. "We'll all be thanking you this winter."

Outside of Trevor's office, Robi led him across the warehouse to another door. Beyond it was a simple bunkhouse with an iron stove for heat and cooking as well as eight cots with footlockers beside them. Six of the cots were currently occupied by four men and two women. None of them showed any sign of magic, which suggested they were pure warriors. If that was so, it was no wonder they were having such a hard time with the demons and monsters outside.

"Alright, you lot," Robi said. "We've got a new recruit, a scout. We're making a run and Ronin here will be guiding us around any trouble. He can also enchant our weapons so we can actually hurt any demons we can't avoid."

Danny offered a polite nod. "Pleasure to meet you all. Are there any other magic users among the group?"

One of the women—she looked like more of a girl with

her slight build and green robes—raised a hesitant hand. "I can do a little magic. I serve Adonael, but I'm not strong enough to enchant weapons. I can heal wounds and negate poison."

"Edith is a new member of the team," Robi said. "She joined about a month ago. After we got rescued by the hero and his companions, I decided we needed a healer of our own. Edith was willing to join. Did I tell you I met the hero? I even shook his hand."

Danny grinned. "Wow. I never had the honor myself."

Robi shook his head. "I was gutted when the Crown announced his death. Unlikely as it seemed, I'd hoped for a chance to repay him for saving me."

His genuine sentiment warmed Danny's heart. It was nice to know his efforts had meant something to someone. Still, he kept his expression carefully under control when he said, "As the hero, saving people was his job. But I bet he'd be glad to know you appreciated it."

"I suppose that will have to be enough." Robi gave a full-body shake. "Anyway, if we're going to be fighting together, we'd best talk a little strategy. Can you do anything else when you're enchanting our weapons?"

"I can fight," Danny said. "But that's pretty much it for magic."

In fact, Danny could do far more than that magically, but he had no desire to show off even close to his full power. Doing so would lead to far too many questions, none of which he was eager to answer.

Robi nodded. "Figured. Still, if we can hurt the demons, that should give us a fair chance against them as long as there aren't too many. The group we encountered on our earlier trip was pretty small. Granted, they were crimson ogres and we got our asses kicked, but I'm confident we'll do better this time."

"Based on what?" one of the men asked.

"Based on our group now having two new members." Robi nodded toward the speaker. "That's Bertram, our resident pessimist. Rest assured if there's a potential downside to any situation, he'll find it. It's a surprisingly useful trait which has helped us improve many a plan."

"Pleasure," Danny said.

Bertram nodded his shaggy head. Between the beard and the hair about all Danny could see of his face were his eyes, and they were piercing green. He had a warrior's build without being bulky.

"Assuming we run into trouble," Danny said. "What's the standard formation?"

"The fighters surround the wagons with Edith in the center where she can heal anyone that gets injured. You'll protect her and the drivers while you maintain our enchantments." Robi shrugged. "That's about it. Without knowing the exact circumstances, it's impossible to make more specific plans."

"Fair enough," Danny said. Staying in the center would suit him fine. It would let him use some of his more subtle spells to influence the battle without anyone noticing. "Is there anything we need to do before morning? Also, mention was made of stew."

"No, we're good." Robi grinned. "And dinner is served at sunset."

CHAPTER 11

Lyra did a lot of thinking on her way back from Demon King Castle. Based on what Ardent Lilly said, the demon king was regaining her strength far from the Five Kingdoms. Lyra didn't take the demon lord's word for it, but a thorough search of the castle hadn't turned up the slightest clue as to where she'd gone. Given the size of the known world, it was impossible to decide where to begin a search.

At least that was her opinion. Hopefully King Richard would agree. He wasn't always the most reasonable of men, but even he would have to accept reality when it slapped him in the face.

The walk back to Villipan City had been a harrowing one. She'd encountered three groups of mixed monsters and demons. She destroyed the smallest and avoided the other two. Leading a group of hunters to wipe out the cursed things would be a far better use of her time than tracking down nonexistent clues about the demon king. As far as she could tell, the hell portal wasn't summoning any more demons, which meant that once they finished off the ones already wandering the Five Kingdoms, it should be the end of them.

She glanced at the royal castle and smiled at her rare moment of optimism. In truth, she had no idea if her assumptions were right.

Lyra stopped dead in the middle of the street. She'd been so focused on the demon king and invading monsters she'd forgotten all about the churches. If their portals were still open they might be bringing in reinforcements from just about anywhere. While she wasn't as strong as Daniel, she and Eve should be able to seal any still-active portals. They'd need a team of warriors to fight their way to the churches, but surely there was a squad of arcane knights available.

She picked up the pace, hurrying through the busy streets, ignoring the humans who were trying to live their lives as best they could under the circumstances. During her many years among them, Lyra had always been impressed the most by their adaptability. Humans could endure just about anything and come through it with their determination intact. Given the brevity of their lives, it was truly amazing.

The guards on duty at the castle gate didn't even try and slow her down. Probably figured she had important news. They weren't wrong but she did wish the news was better. Inside the keep she paused and expanded her awareness. It was approaching noon, so she assumed Richard would either be in the war room or his private suite.

Sure enough she sensed his presence in the second-floor suite. Lyra hurried to the nearest set of stairs and climbed. A couple twists and turns brought her to the hall that led to the royal suite. Outside the door stood four guards, all of them glowing with magic. Arcane knights then. What could've happened to compel the king to waste the time of four of the kingdom's best warriors like this?

It seemed she wasn't the only one with news to share.

When the knights saw her approaching, one of them slumped with relief. "Lady Shael, please tell me you have good news. His Majesty has been terribly anxious since the demon appeared."

"What demon?" Lyra asked.

"I'm not certain what sort it was, but a demon approached the walls while the king and crown prince were inspecting the troops. A passing wizard destroyed it before it had a chance to attack, but the king fears it was sent to assassinate him. Given what happened in Forte I'm not sure he's wrong."

"It couldn't have been very strong if a random wizard had the power to destroy it. It may well have been an imp sent to spy on the capital. Has the wizard responsible been located?"

"No, ma'am. Captain Alard sent a team to search, but no luck so far."

That was strange. Any wizard she'd ever met would be looking for some sort of reward if they slew a demon, especially one so close to the capital. Well, if anyone could figure it out, Alard could. Lyra had great respect for the man.

"Could you announce me?"

"Yes, ma'am." The knight knocked once on the door and stuck his head in. "Lady Shael, Majesty."

"At last. Send her in at once."

The knight pushed the door open all the way and waved Lyra through. The others on duty hadn't spoken a word during their conversation. Two had their eyes closed to better focus on the ether while the other watched the hall in both directions. Clearly they were taking their jobs seriously.

Lyra left them to their work and stepped into the royal suite. King Richard sat at the dining table and waved her into a chair. He looked exhausted; his eyes shadowed and blood-shot, and new streaks of gray in his hair.

"Please tell me you have good news."

"My news is mixed. Demon King Castle is abandoned and the hell gate is no longer producing demons. I searched every room and found no clue as to where the demon king has gone." Lyra steeled herself. "I also spoke to Ardent Lilly."

"What!? How?"

"She's closely connected to this world at the moment. I didn't learn anything useful other than to have her confirm that the demon king isn't in the Five Kingdoms anymore. Mostly she wanted to mock our efforts at victory."

"It does my heart no good to learn that a demon lord is watching our world so closely."

"Since we can't do anything about it, I would put it out of your mind entirely. I did have one thought as I was traveling. It's possible the churches I mentioned are still bringing in more monsters via portal. I think it would be worthwhile for Eve, myself, and a squad of arcane knights to seal them."

"Can you do so without the hero?"

"It will be more difficult," Lyra admitted. "But not impos-sible. At a minimum, I'd like to investigate one and confirm whether it is or isn't portaling in monsters."

Richard nodded. "Good idea. If monsters and demons are appearing faster than we can kill them, our task is impossi-ble. We have one squad of reserve arcane knights in the city. Take them and Eve and do what you can. May Adonael guide you."

"May she guide us all."

○

E
ve's knees ached as she knelt in front of the altar. She spent a lot of time praying in the cathedral's chapel. Hoping, in vain so far, that she might get another oracle from Adonael. Despite her daily entreaties the archangel continued to ignore the pleas of her high priestess. Eve couldn't help resenting her patron's silence even as she felt guilty about it. The archangel had an entire universe to look after, it wasn't like the problems of a single world were the be all and end all, especially considering how much she'd already done to help them.

She sighed and stood. Tomorrow was Holy Day and she had to figure out what she was going to say to the people. There wasn't a ton of good news even if the city had been peaceful so far. Maybe just the usual general encouragement and then some songs in praise of Adonael. Those were usually popular.

Eve turned toward the door and about jumped out of her skin when she spotted Lady Shael standing a few feet inside the chapel, watching her. "Would it kill you to make a little noise?"

"It might out in the field. Judging by your body language, things aren't going well."

Eve smiled but it felt weak to her. "It's not going so bad all things considered. I just keep hoping Adonael will tell me something else. My hopes, it seems, are doomed to disappointment. What brings you by? I seldom see you even on Holy Day."

"I need your help. I've had the alarming thought that the

churches we found might still be summoning monsters. We need to seal the portals and I can't do it without your help. I've got a team of arcane knights ready to go. Can you leave your duties?"

Eve found the prospect of doing something useful rather than kneeling and hoping incredibly appealing. "I can. Sister Rose is more than competent to handle the weekly service. In fact, given my recent doubts, she might be better. Whenever I talk to her about it, she just says to have faith in Adonael and everything will work out. Is it bad that the high priestess has doubts faith is enough?"

"Faith has its uses, but relying on it is foolish. Heaven helps those who help themselves."

Eve quite liked the sound of that. "Are you sure we can seal the portals without Daniel? It looked like all he could do to force the sword into them."

"I'm sure of absolutely nothing other than we need to do something to stop more of the creatures that are killing people from showing up. Maybe we'll get to the first church and find the portal is inactive. I'm fine with that outcome as well. We can easily pivot to hunting when we're finished."

"Have you let the other kings know?"

Lyra shook her head. "No reason to. Without the hero's sword or some other source of mithril, they wouldn't be able to close them anyway. Miles de Forte is supposed to be here in a couple days. Perhaps he'll have some news of worth. I'm not counting on it given how quickly they were forced to flee their capital. Anyway, we leave at dawn, so be ready."

Eve nodded. "I will be. It feels good to have something to do."

Anything to take her mind off her failures would be welcome.

CHAPTER 12

D anny stood outside the warehouse along with Robi, his team, and two teamsters seated on their respective wagons. Trevor was there as well, but the merchant wouldn't be joining them on this trip. Perhaps he was less confident in Danny's ability as a scout than he said. And that was fine. Danny didn't expect instant trust. As far as everyone knew he was a rookie adventurer with a few useful tricks up his sleeve. It was a reminder that the guild master's advice about getting his elite rank before moving on to bigger and better things was prudent.

Not that Danny needed much convincing. While he was very much determined to figure out how to destroy whatever magic allowed the people of this world to summon someone from his, he was equally determined not to make any foolish mistakes. It wasn't just his life on the line, but the lives of two more innocent people.

Robi clapped him on the shoulder. The group's leader wore mail and heavy leathers. An arming sword was buckled at his waist and his shield hung from his back like a pack. He and his team would be riding in the wagons, so only Danny would be forced to walk.

"Sleep well?" Robi asked.

"Yeah, fine. A cot beats the ground any day of the week. What's the holdup?"

"Master Trevor's scribe is preparing some purchase orders for us. His agent should have everything ready in the village. We just need to compare the purchase orders to the agent's invoices then go to the farms to collect the goods. We're only visiting one town this trip and it shouldn't take more than a week. You nervous?"

"Not especially. I was curious about one thing. The guild contract says five gold coins, payable on our safe return, but it implies there would be five wagons. Since you're only sending two and I'll be acting as a scout rather than a guard, does that invalidate the contract?"

"That's a good question. My team is on retainer with the company, which means we don't have a separate contract for each trip. You can trust Master Trevor to do right by you, but if you want clarification, best get it before we leave."

"No, I'm fine with that," Danny said. "I was just curious for future reference. How do contracts ordinarily work?"

"Usually the details are spelled out and you're not required to do any more than what's specified. Most adventurers will go above and beyond the minimum. It's a way to build goodwill for the guild and get repeat clients. But it's not required."

"We'll chalk this up to special circumstances then."

A thin, harried-looking man in a red robe emerged from the warehouse and hurried to Trevor. He carried three scrolls which he handed over.

Robi strode over to Trevor and Danny tagged along. The rest of the team drifted closer as well.

"Okay." Trevor passed the scrolls to Robi. "You're all set. I'm expecting good results. Best of luck."

"You heard the man," Robi said. "Load up. Ronin, you can ride with us until we're outside the city."

"Once we're outside," Danny said. "You'll want to set a slow pace for the first half hour or so to give me a head start. Scouting won't do much good if you follow right on my tail."

"Sure thing." Robi climbed up into the seat of the first wagon beside the driver and Danny got in the back with Edith and Bertram.

When everyone was aboard, they rumbled out into the street toward the city gate. Plenty of heads turned to look at them, some rather pityingly. Probably figured they'd all be monster food by the end of the week. Well, he'd be sure to prove them all wrong. And not just by scouting. He'd been thinking about it the night before. It would be no particular challenge for him to eliminate any small groups of demons he ran into. On his own, he could use the ethersword freely which would make the job much easier. The trick would be to allow enough of the enemy through to make it look like he wasn't doing anything special.

Who would've thought pretending to be weak would be so tricky?

As soon as they were outside the wall, Danny hopped to the ground and said, "Barring any issues, I'll see you all around noon."

He waved, activated his stealth field, and ran down the road at a brisk trot. At half a mile he picked up speed. Danny wanted to have a look at the road for a good ways ahead. Given the lack of attacks on Rosenbar, he assumed the local area was secure. Of course, for all he knew a squad of demons was just waiting for someone dumb enough to step beyond the walls. Best to take nothing for granted.

He ran for a couple of hours, every sense alert for any sign of corruption. At the top of a little hill he stopped for the first time. There was nothing dangerous within range of his perception. As expected, the demons were focusing further away from the large population centers. It was a cruel but clever strategy. Kill the farmers, destroy the crops and livestock, and let the city people starve during the winter. When they were too weak to fight, the demons could stroll in and kill them all at their leisure.

Danny looked out over the rolling hills and valleys. It was a beautiful place. He wasn't bitter enough to deny that. The people he'd met in Rosenbar seemed decent enough. In fact, outside of the royal family and their pet elf, everyone he'd met was okay. Until he was ready to leave on his quest, Danny determined to do the best he could to help them all survive.

After catching his breath, he jogged another five miles without encountering anything remotely threatening. Ten miles should be far enough for the morning. If they hadn't caught up before it got close to noon, Danny would back-track until he joined up with the caravan.

He was about to settle in under an oak tree to rest when he caught the faint presence of corruption. It was very weak. Turning slowly, he tried to orient on it. What he sensed was well off the road and moving generally parallel to it. Toward the caravan.

As soon as he figured that out he rushed back the way he'd come. This would be the perfect chance for them to fight together.

○

Danny spotted the wagons about an hour after he started running back. He'd left the source of corruption behind a little while ago. In truth, he wasn't even sure it was headed for the caravan though he couldn't imagine a demon, assuming it sensed a group of humans, not attacking. Unless it had another order it was following, which wasn't impossible.

At a hundred yards out, Danny slowed and let his stealth field fade away. When he got closer the drivers reined in.

"How's the road?" Robi asked.

"Clear for another few miles. But I sensed a demon and decided to backtrack and let you know. It was traveling this way parallel to the road. It may turn aside before reaching us, but I wanted to be here in case it doesn't."

"Good decision," Robi said. "It's close enough to stop for the noon break. Let's rest and see if anything nasty decides to pay us a visit. You must be tired, have a seat while we keep watch."

"Thanks." Danny jumped up and sat on the driver's seat of the first wagon beside Robi while the teamster got down to check on the horses. It was probably unnecessary, but Danny cast a subtle protective spell on both drivers. It wouldn't stop a truly determined attack, but might buy them some time if something snuck past Danny.

"How strong of a demon was it?" Edith asked in a trembling voice.

"Not really strong judging by its aura of corruption. But even a weak demon isn't something to overlook."

"I would never underestimate a demon," Edith hastened to add.

"Horses are holding up well, sir," the driver said.

"Good," Robi said. "Let's break out a quick bite to eat. We'll need all our strength if—"

Danny raised a hand, cutting him off. "It's coming."

Robi had his sword out in an instant. "Where?"

Danny pointed to the left side of the road. It was the same demon he'd sensed before. As far as he could tell it was alone. But even a weak demon could camouflage the presence of lesser monsters. Assuming there was only one enemy might prove fatal.

"About two hundred yards out and closing." Danny concentrated and the others' weapons glowed white with holy energy. "That should come in handy, but don't get careless."

Fifty feet out the demon shimmered into view. It looked like a crimson ogre: about eight feet tall, heavily muscled, reddish skin. The main difference was the glowing red eyes. Someone had turned it into a thrall. But thralls generally couldn't turn invisible or sneak up on people. They just charged in and fought until you killed them.

Or so Lyra had told him. This thing must be something else.

Robi and the other warriors formed an arc in front of the wagons while the drivers joined Danny and Edith in the bed of the first. Edith's hands were shaking and both drivers were muttering prayers to Adonael. Had they not been present when Danny and his companions had rescued Trevor? He couldn't remember but assumed not. That had been a much scarier situation.

The thrall charged, ending his speculation.

When it was five strides away, Danny conjured a little block of pure telekinetic force in front of its foot. The thrall stumbled and Robi chose that moment to dart in and slash it across the chest. His holy magic enhanced sword cut a deep groove across the thrall's right pec.

The blow didn't faze the creature in the least and it waded in, fists leading.

Robi jumped back, avoiding a right cross. Bertram took the opportunity to slam his ax into the overextended arm and chop it off at the elbow.

The rest of the team made their moves. Swords stabbed and slashed and soon the thrall was reduced to a pile of unmoving flesh, the corruption burned out of it.

"We're in the clear," Danny said. "I can't sense any more corruption. You guys fought impressively."

Robi sheathed his sword. "Only because of your enhancement magic. I wasn't sure how effective it would be, but that was outstanding."

"It was just a little boost but thank you. If you'll move away, I'll take care of the remains."

"Why bother?" asked the other female adventurer—Danny was pretty sure her name was Melia. "The thing's dead."

"True, but if a skilled necromancer should find the remains, they could get up to no good with them. Better if I burn them just to be sure. Don't worry, it won't take long."

"Do as you think best," Robi said. "You're the magic user after all."

"Is anyone hurt?" Edith asked.

No one was and after an application of fire magic reduced the thrall to ash, they decided to get moving. That was a good idea since lingering near the battle site would be hard on the horses if not the people. Animals were surprisingly sensitive to such things. It was like they could sense something wrong had happened.

The rest of the day passed without issue and the group finally made camp around half an hour before dark. The process consisted of pulling the wagons off to the side of the road and building a fire for cooking. Edith got busy making soup while the rest of them settled in to rest.

"I'll take first watch," Danny said.

Robi shook his head. "We'll be handling the watch rotation. You need your rest. If anything happens tomorrow, we'll be counting on your magic."

"That was amazing earlier. My sword actually felt lighter thanks to your magic. I'm Martin, by the way. I don't think we've been properly introduced."

"Everything happened quite quickly. I'm Ronin." Danny shook hands with the slim, whip of a man. "Holy magic can have that effect. It isn't so much the weapon getting lighter but that your life force is resonating with the holy energy, making you stronger."

"Is holy magic your specialty?" Melia asked. "I would've guessed illusion given your skill with stealth."

"I don't have a specialty. My teacher insisted I learn a bit of everything. Specialists tend to have blind spots and he wanted to protect me from that."

"I never thought about that," Robi said. "We've never worked with a wizard on the team. You certainly bring a unique perspective."

"I do my best. This is my first time working with other adventurers, so if I do anything wrong, I hope I can count on you all to sort me out."

"All newbies screw up, it's part of the learning process," Bertram said. "We'll do our best to steer you right."

Danny smiled. "I appreciate that. How much further until our pickup?"

"If we don't run into any unpleasantness, by the end of the day tomorrow." Robi shrugged. "Can't say I'm excited about our chances of making it on time."

"Better late and alive than dead and on time," Danny said.

Robi barked a laugh. "Can't argue with you there. It's not like anyone's expecting us at a particular time."

"Soup's ready," Edith said.

Danny's mouth watered. A hot meal and a good night's sleep would be just the thing. He planned to place a ward around the camp before bed. It wasn't that he didn't trust his companions to keep watch, but under the current circumstances, taking undue risks would be foolish in the extreme. An invisible demon could sneak right up on a guard—if that wasn't a thought to keep you awake at night he didn't know what was—but nothing could sneak past his magic.

CHAPTER 13

When Danny woke, the final member of the team was on guard duty. While it wasn't a big deal, Robi hadn't done a very good job introducing everyone. He wondered why for a moment but when the likely answer came to him he found it rather depressing. Robi probably figured Danny was going to get killed while scouting and he didn't want his people getting too attached. He couldn't even blame the guy. For anyone else, being a scout, out in the field alone, was about the most dangerous job in the Five Kingdoms right now.

"Morning." Danny spoke softly so as not to wake the others. The sun wasn't even up yet so he saw no reason to bother them. "We weren't introduced yesterday, I'm Ronin."

The man looked at him, shook his head, and pointed at his throat before making a couple of gestures Danny didn't understand.

"You're mute?" he asked.

The man nodded.

Swell, they had a mute guy on guard duty. If something

showed up, how the hell was he supposed to wake everyone up?

That's when Danny noticed the iron triangle on the ground beside him. That would certainly do the job. It still seemed like a bad idea. Having someone unable to shout a warning if some enemy was sneaking up behind you would be a problem in a fight. Of course, given the number of adventurers willing to step out from behind the city walls, Robi wasn't in a position to be fussy.

Danny left the silent guard to his work and stoked the fire. The least he could do was make breakfast for everyone. Not that it would be anything special given their supplies. He settled on beans, bacon, and fried bread. He needed to make a pretty big batch for all of them. By the time he was nearly done, the sun was peeking over the horizon and everyone had begun to stir under their blankets.

The smell of sizzling bacon must have finished the job as they all soon sat up and looked toward the fire. Danny waved. "Morning, everyone. Breakfast is almost ready."

"You can cook too?" Melia said. "Are you looking for a wife by any chance?"

"No, but if that changes, I'll keep you in mind. And warming up a few ingredients isn't exactly fine dining. Still, a hot meal isn't a terrible way to start the morning. I figure we've got another long day ahead of us, might as well face it with a full stomach."

"I can't argue with your logic," Robi said. "Though if you keep doing so much work, you'll shame the rest of us."

"In my experience, the new guy generally works hard to make a good impression. Besides, I was already awake."

Danny dished up the food and they ate in companionable silence. When the last bowl had been wiped clean, Edith hurried to collect them and started cleaning. The teamsters worked on hitching up the horses. Danny was happy to stay out of their way. He knew how to ride a horse, but apparently his host hadn't learned anything about wagons. Unless there was a deuce and a half around here for him to drive, Danny wasn't going to be much help with transportation.

Robi shifted to stand beside him. "You good to go again?"

"Yeah, sure. I slept like a rock and now I'm full. What more could I need?"

Robi smiled. "You've got a good attitude, I appreciate that. I worried the stress might be getting to you. Keeping us from walking into something is a big responsibility."

"I'm doing my best. At the end of the day, that's all any of us can do. Hopefully it'll be good enough."

"Having seen your performance so far, I'm sure it will be." Robi glanced over at the wagons. "Looks like they're about ready. You might as well head out. Be sure and come back at the first sign of trouble. Don't do anything crazy."

Danny pushed away from the tree he'd been leaning against. "Have no fear on that account. I'm no hero."

"We'll plan to meet up at the first intersection," Robi said. "That's where we turn off for the village."

Danny gave a thumbs-up. It surprised him when he learned the gesture meant the same thing in both worlds. He jogged a little ways down the road then activated his stealth field. So far, the job was going smoothly. On the one hand that was good, but on the other, Danny never trusted it. He'd seen too many missions go sideways when you got comfortable.

The hours passed slowly as he jogged along. There was no hint of corruption within his range. Despite what he'd heard about demon activity, the Five Kingdoms covered a huge area. The odds of actually running into a demon on any given day had to be small.

He cursed himself. Never think something like that; it was just asking for trouble.

And sure enough, not half an hour later Danny sensed a demonic presence—no, multiple presences, all of them stronger than the thrall they'd killed the day before. He stopped and honed in on them. About fifty yards ahead and off to the side of the road. Now that he knew what to look for, it was easy to spot the ethereal outlines of their invisible figures.

Lucky for Danny, low-tier demons were nowhere near as good at stealth as he was. On the downside, he couldn't tell what sort of demons they were. Well, that was fine. Whatever they turned out to be, he could tell they were no match for him.

He opened his storage, pulled out the ethersword, and lowered his stealth field. No sense using stealth magic while holding mithril. The demons would sense it no matter what he did. As with all things in life there were tradeoffs. In this case he was happy to trade stealth for power.

Holding the deactivated ethersword in his right hand, Danny strolled down the road in plain view. Time to see if the demons were stupid enough to attack someone carrying mithril, even if he was a lone human.

Turned out they were every bit as stupid as Danny hoped. Five lamprey-headed demons came roaring toward him.

In the blink of an eye, he activated the ethersword and max physical enhancement. A single swing of the white blade sliced a demon in half.

Moving so fast he'd be invisible to anyone watching, Danny reduced the demons to rapidly evaporating puddles of black goo. He was delighted to see that the ethersword was every bit as effective as the mithril katana. A moment of careful study confirmed that he'd eliminated all the threats.

Satisfied with his work, he extinguished the blade and put the hilt back in storage. Business complete, he turned invisible and trotted on.

An hour and a half before noon, Danny reached the turnoff Robi mentioned. It was a hard-packed dirt road like the one they'd been following only a little narrower. There wasn't even a sign with its name. On the maps he'd studied, few of the roads had names. Only the trade roads, and they were named after the direction they ran. This one being the Northwestern Trade Road. That had to make it hard to give people directions.

He shook his head and put this world's naming idiosyncrasies out of his mind. If it worked for them, what did he care?

Most of an hour later the wagons came rolling up to the turnoff. From the tightness in their expressions, it looked like they were anxious about something. Danny sensed nothing, so he couldn't imagine what had them worked up.

Robi hopped to his feet. "Are you okay?"

Danny cocked his head. "Fine, why?"

"We passed what looked like the site of a battle. The remains of some demons had nearly finished dissolving. I feared you might have gotten caught up in a fight."

"No. Someone killed them, probably not long before I passed through, but I saw no sign of whoever did it. I'd say I missed them by twenty minutes. Likely some arcane knights on patrol."

Robi blew out a breath. "Right, lucky for us then. We'll

take a short break then get moving. I want to reach the village before dark."

○

I t was a little over an hour until sunset when Danny spotted the walled village. It wasn't on fire and he heard no screams. That was a good sign. He could also sense many life forces moving around. All around the village were sprawling fields of what he guessed was wheat. He was far from an agricultural expert, but the fields looked healthy. The distant figures of farmers moving through them indicated that the locals had no concerns at the moment.

Danny frowned. Word must've gotten to them about the dangers, right? He'd assumed so, but given the decidedly worthless means of mass communications on this world, maybe he'd assumed wrong. The best way to come up with an answer was to ask a simple question: Did those in power benefit from the regular folks knowing the truth? In this case he wasn't sure, but he did take some small comfort that this particular truth remained the same both on Earth and Valindor.

He shrugged and sat on the side of the road to wait for the wagons to catch up. It was a beautiful summer day and Danny was content to enjoy the sunshine.

The creak of approaching wheels startled him from a light doze. He hadn't been asleep, just resting his eyes. With a yawn Danny stood and canceled his stealth field. The rest of the group was approaching at a walk. Robi waved to him and Danny waved back. As the wagon passed he grabbed a sideboard and swung up beside Robi.

"A peaceful day," Robi said.

Danny grimaced. "Don't say that. You're tempting fate. These people seem to have no idea the sort of danger they're facing. Do we tell them or just stick to business?"

"Stick to business. We're being paid to collect crops and bring them back, not act as Crown criers. I have no desire to answer the no-doubt-many questions the news would prompt."

He had no argument for that and even if he did, this was Robi's show. Danny was just along to make sure they didn't get ambushed. "Any chance of a bed and a hot meal tonight?"

"This town has a tavern, but no inn. We can probably find a nice pile of hay to serve as a bed. On the plus side, Master Trevor provided me with some coin to cover our food and other expenses."

"I never turn down free food and hay is better than the ground." At least it was if you had a good bedroll to spread over it. If you didn't, it was worse since you were constantly getting poked by stray straw.

The wagon trundled along the rest of the way to the village gate. If you could call a pair of battered wagons with sharpened stakes tied to the sides a gate. An ogre wouldn't even slow down at the sight of it, much less a demon.

"This is..." Danny trailed off, not entirely sure how to say what he was thinking in a polite way.

"This is designed to keep out bears and other beasts," Robi said. "And it does the job fine."

Danny doubted a serious bear would be overly impressed either, but he kept his peace.

"Hello!" Robi shouted. "Is anyone on duty?"

A disgruntled-looking man about a hundred pounds overweight and wearing a food-stained white tunic that left the bottom of his belly visible waddled into view. He squinted at the wagons with bloodshot eyes.

"It's getting so a man can't nap in peace anymore," said the guard or whatever he was. "What do you need?"

"We're here to meet with Luis Genin, Master Trevor's agent," Robi said.

The fat man nodded. "Luis's been wondering where you folks were. Can't hardly talk about anything else at the Tankard. He'll be relieved to see you. Ah, shit. Can someone give me a hand moving the wagons?"

"I got it." Danny jumped down, enhanced his strength, and shoved them both out of the way. They were actually pretty light so he had to be careful not to be too rough. "Go ahead."

When the wagons were through Danny asked, "Would you like me to put them back?"

The guard nodded. "I'd be much obliged. For a skinny fella, you're awful strong."

Danny pushed the wagons back in place with equal ease. "I'm an arcane knight. The magic is what makes me strong. Good evening."

He trotted back to the wagons and hopped aboard. Robi was staring at him for some reason. "You can make yourself stronger too?"

"Of course, that's the first thing an arcane knight learns and is the basis for our combat abilities. You literally can't be an arcane knight if you can't do it. You'll get kicked out and forced to become a wizard."

"I didn't know that."

Danny shrugged; that was unsurprising since he'd made it up on the spot. "You've never trained to be an arcane knight, so naturally you wouldn't. Anyway, what's this agent like?"

"Luis is a good guy. Serious about his work, but easy to talk to over a pint. He should have all our cargo lined up, then it'll just be a matter of driving out to the farms and collecting the crates. It won't go that smoothly of course. Never does. But that's fine. As long as we avoid any demons or monsters, I'm happy to put up with a few mundane annoyances."

They rode through the town square—really just a dirt circle in the center of the buildings—and continued on to a simple, single-story building not far from the northern edge of the village. It was nothing special and if not for a shingle engraved with a scale beside the door, Danny wouldn't have given it a second look.

"The scale means money changer, right?" Danny asked. "I thought he was an agent."

"Luis does a bunch of different things. His work for Master Trevor only takes a few hours each month, so not exactly a full-time position."

The drivers guided their wagons to the side of the road and Robi jumped down. "I won't be long."

"Mind if I join you?" Danny asked. "I'm curious to meet this fellow."

Robi shrugged. "Fine with me. The rest of you watch the wagons."

The odds of anyone in the village trying to steal the wagons seemed remote to Danny, but it would give the other adventurers something to do while they were inside.

A quick knock on the door preceded Robi pushing it open and striding in. The main room was nothing special. There was a desk, some hard chairs, a cabinet, and, of greatest interest, a heavy-duty safe. Nothing like the one at the Adventurers' Guild but impressively large all the same.

Behind the desk sat a man straight out of central casting for the part of Scrooge. Old and thin with a severe scowl that made his brows nearly cover his eyes, Luis looked like the sort of person who would send kids running for home with a look.

To Danny's immense surprise, a bright, cheerful voice emerged from that face. "Robi, my boy, I've been worried. Trevor's never been this late sending someone for pickup. Is all well?"

Danny could only stare in dumbfounded silence. There was no way, absolutely none, that Luis didn't know about the demon king. Danny refused to believe it. No matter how terrible the lines of communication were, everyone had to know about that.

"Uh, we have run into a few issues," Robi said, sounding as bemused as Danny felt. "The demon king and his army arrived. They've dispersed throughout the Five Kingdoms and are raising all kinds of hell. The hero did defeat the demon king, but died in the process, so we—and by we I mean the Villipan army—need to clean up the rest. Did you truly hear nothing about it?"

As they were talking, Danny looked into the ether. As he feared, Luis's mind had been manipulated. Lyra could probably figure out the details, but even someone as inexperienced as Danny could tell something had been done to him. The lingering traces of magic made that clear. What he couldn't tell was whether or not it was simple memory manipulation or if he was still under the effects of mind control.

"No one saw fit to tell us anything," Luis said. "And as far as I know, the area is peaceful. Maybe the demons just haven't gotten to us yet. Adonael be praised. So, how many wagons did you bring?"

"Only two," Robi said. "This was a test run to see if we could make it through safely. We'll take as much as we can this trip then be back in a week or so. How was the harvest?"

"Good. We've got more summer vegetables than you can shake a stick at. The grain fields are also in perfect condition. We should get a banner yield this fall."

"That's the best news I've heard in a month." Robi held out his order contracts. "I trust you've got purchase invoices for me."

Luis opened his desk drawer and pulled out three sheets of parchment. "There you are. Those are enough to fill two wagons. When you get back, I've got twice as many ready to go so be sure to bring more wagons."

Robi took the invoices, compared them to his contracts and nodded. "I'll do that, thanks, Luis."

Luis nodded and shifted his gaze to Danny. "Are you going to introduce me to your companion? I know the others, but this is a new face."

"Right, sorry. Luis, this is Ronin, our scout. He's the reason we made it here safe and sound."

Danny nodded. "Pleasure, sir."

"Likewise, young man. It's always good to meet someone trying to make the world a better place. But do be careful. You've chosen a dangerous occupation."

Danny smiled. Compared to being the hero, this was a piece of cake. "I will be, sir, thank you. It's late, so we should get settled for the night and a visit to that tavern you mentioned wouldn't go amiss."

Robi chuckled. "I imagine the others would agree. Until next time, Luis."

Luis waved them out and bent his head back to whatever he'd been working on. As far as Danny could tell, whatever magic was lingering in his brain didn't react to them. What it meant, he was less certain of.

As soon as they were outside Robi sighed. "Can you believe that? This place has been living a peaceful, ignorant life while everywhere else is chaos. What are the odds?"

"Zero," Danny said. "His mind has been manipulated. I'm not sure exactly how, but I can see something. I fear this peaceful little town may have been subjected to some demonic meddling. What I'm less certain of is whether or not it's ongoing."

"If you're joking it's in terrible taste."

"I wish I were. I wish everything was as peaceful here as it looks. But I'm not and it isn't. We need to keep it quiet while I check a few more people. I should've started with the guard, but I was so distracted by the gate and his looks I didn't even think of it. The tavern should be the perfect place to investigate. If Luis is the only one that's been messed with, then we can assume the problem is outside the village. If it's more widespread then the problem is likely in the village itself."

"How do you know all this?" Robi somehow managed to look both worried and incredulous.

Right, Danny was supposed to be a newly minted adventurer with basically no experience. Getting out of character was potentially a problem, but not as big a one as keeping silent about what was going on.

"I don't know anything for sure, these are just guesses based on what I see. I might be totally wrong about the cause of the magic, but I'm not wrong about it being there."

"Hey, you two!" Bertram said. "What's the holdup? I need a drink in the worst way."

Robi glanced at Danny. "Should I tell them?"

"Don't ask me. You know your team better than I do."

"Right. Okay, I'll wait until after we eat. You'll know more by then anyway, right?"

"At a minimum I'll have a fair idea how badly the town has been undermined. Though of course I still won't know all the details."

"That's a start. We'll talk after dinner and before we sleep."

Robi's panic didn't fill Danny with confidence. What he wouldn't give to have Lyra and his companions with him right now.

But he didn't and that was the end of it. Somehow he'd have to survive whatever they'd walked into with the people he had on hand. Whether he could do it without giving himself away was another matter altogether.

CHAPTER 14

Lyra would be happy to never set foot in Fell Forest again. Every time she visited the cursed woods something awful happened. For example, right now, one of the arcane knights that had accompanied her and Eve on their mission was being aggressively and loudly sick behind a mutated tree. The five human knights—Lyra hadn't bothered learning their names—were relatively young and inexperienced. Not her first choice for reinforcements, but when you had nothing better available, you made do.

She'd led her team into the forest northeast of Rosenbar near where, based on the two churches they'd found so far, she assumed the next one would be. That had been a couple of hours ago and she'd sensed nothing so far. They also hadn't been attacked by monsters or demons. It was too soon to call the mission a failure, but her optimism wasn't over-flowing.

"I'm not sure what's wrong with him," Eve said. "I've been maintaining everyone's protective aura and the corruption doesn't seem as bad now."

"Some people are more sensitive to it than others. He is one such." Lyra suppressed a grimace and sighed. They would need the warriors soon enough, no reason to antagonize them.

"I didn't know that," Eve said. "What causes it?"

Lyra shrugged. "No clue. It's like being born with an extra finger. It just happens sometimes."

"I've never met anyone with an extra finger."

"You're still young."

The valiant knight staggered back into the little clearing where they'd paused to let him empty his stomach. He looked rather pale and weak. Lyra debated sending him back, but figured that on his own he was more apt to get killed.

Eve hurried over and cast a healing spell on him. As the magic took effect, he straightened and said, "Thank you, Lady Carre. I apologize for the unseemly display."

"You can't help it if you're sick." Eve smiled at him with genuine kindness. Lyra didn't know how she managed.

"Let's get moving," Lyra said. "The church can't be too far away."

She tried to sound confident, but the truth was, she had no idea if they'd even find another church. Everything she'd done since learning the demon king was still alive amounted to her best guesses. This was totally uncharted territory for everyone.

They set out with Lyra in the lead. She held the hero's sword at the ready. It was strange wielding it herself. She'd never done so in all her years of training heroes. Doing so felt... disrespectful wasn't quite the right word, but maybe wrong. But however she felt about it, Lyra would do what was necessary. She always did.

"Is it strange that we haven't seen any demons?" Eve whispered.

"No need to stay quiet." She didn't look back at the knights stomping around in their armor, but only a deaf monster wouldn't hear them coming from a mile away. "And yes, it is strange. The corruption hasn't thinned enough to say so, yet the forest appears largely free of enemies. That makes me think they've all been ordered into Villipan."

"That's not very encouraging."

Lyra had never been much good at offering encouragement and didn't even bother trying most of the time.

Half an hour of marching passed without comment when finally Lyra sensed something. It was the first collection of concentrated corruption she'd detected since they entered the forest. Maybe it was a church and maybe it wasn't, but at a minimum it was something different and that warranted a look.

She adjusted her course to lead them right to whatever she'd sensed. Other than the crunching of the knights' steps, the silence of the forest was unnerving. It was all in her head of course. Fell Forest wasn't like a normal forest. Birds and other small animals would be killed in hours if exposed to this much corruption. Only demons, monsters, and mutated beasts lived here.

It didn't take long to reach the source and, sure enough, it was another of the black churches and there wasn't a guard to be found. It was all so wrong.

"Lady Shael?" Eve said.

Lyra shook her head. She had no explanations to offer. "Let's move closer. Defensive formation. Weapons out and extra alert."

She had to give the knights credit. They obeyed her

order, forming a circle around her and Eve with quick, precise movements. Perhaps she'd been too hard on them.

They crossed the open space separating the church from the forest without issue. The lead knight reached for the door, but Lyra stopped him.

"It might be trapped." A couple flicks of the hero's sword reduced the door to scrap. No spells lashed out and nothing appeared to attack them. She almost wished something would just to make this feel normal.

Inside the church they found the black portal in the same spot as the others. The priestess she expected was also absent. It looked like the church had been abandoned.

"Watch the door," Lyra said. "We still need to seal the portal."

The knights shifted and formed a wall between them and the entrance. Lyra and Eve moved closer to the portal. She examined it through the ether. Without question it was still active.

No sense worrying about it. "Ready?"

Eve nodded. "As I'll ever be."

Lyra put the tip of the hero's sword on the portal and pushed with all her might.

Nothing.

Even with full physical enhancement active she couldn't force the blade into the portal.

"Channel divine energy into the sword," Lyra said. "Maybe that will help."

Pure white light ran down the blade and splashed against the portal. Lyra bore down again, trying with all her will and might to force the tip through. But it was no use and after a minute she was forced to give in. She just didn't have strength enough.

"What are we going to do now?"

"I don't know," Lyra said.

But that was a lie. She knew what she had to do. She had to find Daniel and convince him to help her close the portals. Given how he felt about her and that she had no idea where he was at the moment, it was a big job. But however big it might be, she saw no other option.

CHAPTER 15

After dropping off their wagons and horses at an impressively large stable, Danny and the others headed for the village tavern, a rather unimpressive, oversized shack called The Empty Tankard. He and Robi still hadn't mentioned anything about Luis's mind being altered. It wasn't the choice Danny would've made—keeping important information from your team never ended well—but it also wasn't his call. All Danny had to focus on was checking the other villagers to see if they'd been messed with as well.

It wasn't quite pitch black out, but the faint glow on the horizon would be gone soon. The street between the stable and tavern was empty—Danny assumed—because everyone was already drinking.

"Man, I'm so thirsty," Bertram said. "I'm going to get drunk."

"No, you're not," Robi said. "We're on a mission and drinking on Master Trevor's coin. Two mugs each and that's it."

Bertram looked like he wanted to argue, but a single hard look from Robi shut him up. Under the current circumstances, getting drunk was a terrible idea and Danny wholeheartedly approved of Robi shutting it down quickly.

The tavern door hung slightly askew, letting light from inside leak out all around the frame. They pushed through and, just as Danny figured, found the place packed. A whole hog roasted over a raised fire pit in the center of the common room, filling the air with a mix of savory meat smells and smoke. People laughed and joked, seemingly having a great time. Robi led them over to a pair of empty tables on the far right of the room. It would be a tight fit, but they had few options.

As they wove their way past the diners, Danny looked at them through the ether. Sure enough, magic much like whatever was used on Luis glowed in their brains. It didn't seem to be doing them any harm, but that was a small comfort.

Danny caught Robi's eye as they sat and gave a little nod. A slight twist of his lips was the only sign he gave.

"Looks like pork for dinner," Martin said. "I can't wait."

Edith smiled and turned to Danny. "You wouldn't think it, but Martin can outeat all of us."

"I certainly wouldn't have." Though why he should be surprised was another question. A lot of the professional eaters back on Earth were skinny little guys.

He was still pondering this mystery when he sensed corruption approaching. Danny shifted to see the waitress headed their way. She was drop-dead gorgeous with a figure a model would kill for. That was his first clue something was wrong. He activated anti-psychic magic and slipped his dagger out of its sheath.

"What can I get you?" she asked.

Danny swung hard, adding an aura of holy magic as he did so. The dagger sank into her skull up to the hilt. The beautiful blond woman vanished, replaced by a rapidly dissolving succubus. All around him people were moaning and thrashing in their seats.

The team leapt to their feet and drew their weapons.

"What the hell's going on?" Melia asked.

"Killing the demon triggered whatever psychic magic was placed on the villagers," Danny said. "I don't know what it's going to make them do, but we'd best get out of here before they start doing it."

The group scrambled for the door with Danny in the lead. Outside, villagers were emerging from their homes and shuffling around like a bunch of zombies. They weren't actually zombies. Danny could sense their life forces. Which made the problem worse. If they were undead, he could cut them down without a second thought, but the villagers were just victims of the demon's sorcery. Killing them would be wrong, but it might also be necessary for the group to survive.

"What are we going to do?" Martin had his sword at the ready, but seemed as reluctant to use it as Danny.

Everyone looked to Robi, but before he could reply a female voice said, "If only you hadn't noticed my succubus. This would've gone so much easier for everyone."

They all turned back toward the tavern. One of Ardent Lilly's sexy nuns stood on the roof. She carried a black whip that burned with crimson flames and gave off an aura of corruption stronger than the demon's.

"We need to get out of here," Robi said.

More of the zombie-looking villagers were shambling out of the tavern. By Danny's quick estimate there were at least sixty people in the street and the team was surrounded.

"That's going to be a problem," Danny said.

The group shifted away from the tavern zombies but that only moved them closer to the ones from up the street. Their options were going to be kill or be killed in short order.

"I can open a path," Danny said. "We'll hole up in the stable for now."

When no one argued, he pictured a wall of flames springing up between the villagers then splitting in half to form a corridor. Mind controlled or not, living people shied away from fire.

They seized the moment and ran.

"You can't escape me!" The evil nun's laughter chased them all the way back to the stable.

Once they were inside, they shoved the wagons up against the doors. That was far from a permanent solution, but it should buy them a little time.

"What in the nine flaming hells is going on?" Bertram asked. "Who's that woman and what's wrong with the villagers?"

"The woman is a priestess of Ardent Lilly," Edith said. "She has to be controlling the villagers with psychic magic. Doing that requires a lot of power."

"The demon was no doubt helping," Danny said. He was relieved Edith had stepped in to explain about the nun. If Danny had done it, there would've been questions he preferred not to answer. "I need to take her out if we're going to have any chance."

"What do you mean 'you'?" Robi asked. "You can't beat her in a fight."

"I don't plan to fight. I'm going to sneak up behind her

using my stealth field and cut her head off. Unless someone has a better idea, I think it's our best chance. The only other option I see is killing all the villagers. I can only speak for myself, but that plan doesn't sit well with me."

"Can you do it?" Robi asked.

"I don't know." Danny tried to sound less confident than he felt. After the demon king, he doubted one of the nuns would be a problem. "I just know it's our best chance."

Finally, Robi nodded. "What can we do to help?"

"Stay here and be targets. As long as she's focused on you, she'll be less likely to notice me."

Something crashed into the door. The time for debate was over.

Danny climbed into the back of a wagon and jumped up to grab a rafter. He chinned himself up, stood, drew a circle of ether, and set it spinning. It took only a moment to slice a perfect disk out of the roof. Danny activated his stealth field and climbed through.

He slid silently to the edge of the roof and dropped to the ground. Next, it was simply a matter of circling the mob and coming up behind the nun. He pulled the ethersword out of storage. Should be safe enough to use it with the others out of sight. The mithril was tricky, but Danny hoped his stealth field would keep her from sensing it before he was close enough to strike.

He rounded a corner and stepped out into the street.

And found the nun staring right at him. "You're clearly less pathetic than the rest of the trash, but Ardent Lilly grants me the power to see through illusions."

Danny let the stealth field fade away then lit the ethersword. Assassination was out so he was going to have to do this the hard way. "I don't suppose I can convince you to release these people and surrender?"

Her bloodred lips curled up in a sexy smile. "No, but I might let *you* surrender to serve as my personal plaything and footstool."

It seemed they weren't going to come to terms.

Danny activated his physical enhancement and charged.

The priestess cracked her whip, sending a gout of hellfire streaking in at him.

Danny dodged and swung his sword. To his shock, the whip blocked his blow, though he did force the nun back a pace.

He swung twice more and twice more his magical blade was turned aside. It was impressive and worrisome all at the same time.

A stream of hellfire forced him to dive and roll. He came to his feet right in front of the nun and swung his fist as hard as he could. The mithril basket hilt slammed into her head and sent her flying across the road to crash into one of the houses, smashing the wall in.

Danny stared as she climbed back to her feet. The nun didn't speak. Likely because her jaw was only attached to her face by a thin strip of flesh. That blow should've turned her head into pulp. How could she be this strong?

Or had he gotten weaker?

It didn't matter. He needed to finish it before the villagers reached his companions.

He lunged in, sword leading.

Her whip lashed out, knocking him to the side.

Danny used the momentum, spun, and sliced right through her neck. Her head hit the ground with a moist plop.

Further down the road, all the villagers dropped like puppets with their strings cut. Looked like that eliminated the threat.

He extinguished the ethersword and put it back in storage. Next a stream of blazing white flames reduced the nun to ash. He was just finishing up when the rest of the adventurers along with the two least lucky teamsters in history came running his way.

"What happened?" Robi asked. "It sounded like a battle."

"I didn't take her out with the first blow. Luckily it did weaken her enough for me to end it. Are you all okay?"

"Sure, no problem." Robi's look was filled with questions, but Danny had no intention of elaborating.

"What do we do now?" Martin gestured at the unconscious villagers lying around like a bunch of corpses. "How long are they going to stay like this?"

Danny shook his head and walked over to the nearest villager. The control spell was still present, just inactive. If another priestess or even a demon showed up, the people would end up as puppets again. The worst part was, for all his raw power, Danny had no talent for fine work like removing those spells.

"We can bring them back to the Temple of Adonael," Edith said. "The priests will be able to help them."

Bertram cocked his head. "What, you mean load them into the wagons like merchandise? Is that safe?"

"I'm more worried about what might happen if there's someone loyal to Ardent Lilly in Rosenbar," Danny said. "If they reactivate the spell, we'd have over a hundred living puppets in the city to deal with. Which is not a prospect that excites me. And I doubt the people in charge would disagree."

Robi stared at him, jaw bunching and relaxing as he

ground his teeth. He didn't seem to like Danny's reasoning even as he understood it was the truth.

"Maybe we don't have to bring them into the city." Danny focused on Edith, who shrunk under his gaze. "If we brought them close, would the priests come out and treat them?"

Edith's face lit up. "I'm sure they would. Serving and protecting the people is our highest calling. If they can be of service, the priests won't hesitate to help."

Danny offered a little smile. "Now we just need to see if everyone will fit in the wagons. We should probably check the nearby farms as well. If the priestess went this far, I doubt she spared those outside the village. I can do that while the rest of you start loading everyone."

"Sounds like we have a plan," Robi said. "Though Master Trevor isn't going to be happy."

Danny frowned. "I admit I don't know Trevor as well as you, but do you think he'll be upset that we chose to help these people rather than bring back vegetables?"

"Less upset than disappointed," Robi said. "He's been eager to collect supplies and get them in the warehouse for weeks. This will be one more delay. Still, given our choices, there's only one thing we can do. And the sooner we get started, the better."

"Then maybe we can get some of that pork," Martin said.

"Best wait until I get back so I can check it for poison," Danny said.

The blood drained out of Martin's face. "If a demon was cooking it, I suppose that's possible. I'll be sure to wait."

Danny nodded and headed to the gate. Hopefully he wouldn't find a bunch of unconscious farmers to go with their collection of unconscious villagers.

CHAPTER 16

Danny couldn't begin to express how relieved he was to be back within sight of Rosenbar. As he'd feared, the people at every farm within five miles of the nameless village had been in the exact same state as the villagers. That ended up being another forty people they needed to transport. The only good thing was that he found two more wagons and horses to pull them. The teamsters got them ready then Bertram and Martin drove.

Their inexperience combined with the need to care for the afflicted meant the journey back took twice as long as the trip out. The villagers would eat or drink if you put food in their hands, but nothing more. If that hadn't worked the group would've been delivering bodies.

The wagons trundled up beside him and Robi said, "Heaven's mercy. I can't believe we made it all the way back without running into any demons. Adonael must have been watching over us."

Danny had no idea what the archangel was doing, but he

had wiped out two groups of ogres and disintegrated their bodies before the wagons reached them. All things considered, he hadn't felt like playing with monsters.

Danny made the halo symbol. "Looks like. I sense no corruption around here. Would you like me to escort Edith to Adonael's temple?"

Robi thought for a moment then nodded. "Good idea. The sooner we can get these people into the care of those able to help them, the better. And thanks, for everything. We wouldn't have made it without your magic."

Danny grinned. "That's what it means to be part of a team. We all do our best so everyone makes it home."

"Yeah, that's the ideal. But I've heard stories of people cutting and running, leaving their teammates behind to die. It's always an ugly story. Glad it's one I won't have to tell." Robi looked back over his shoulder. "Edith!"

The priestess climbed down from her wagon and hurried over. "Yes?"

"You're going ahead with Ronin to let the temple know what happened. We'll stop a hundred yards out just to make sure the guards don't get nervous."

"Got it." She turned to Danny. "Ready?"

He nodded and they set out at a quick walk. He stayed at an easy pace but didn't dawdle. Just because he couldn't sense any threats at the moment didn't mean something nasty wouldn't show up later.

"If I go too fast," Danny said. "Please let me know."

"I'm not as frail as everyone thinks," Edith said. "I'll be fine."

"I apologize if I did anything to offend you. You're just so small and quiet it's easy to make assumptions."

"It's fine. I'm used to it at this point. Mother always said I need to be more assertive, but it doesn't come naturally. One of the reasons I left the temple to become an adventurer was the hope that it would help me get brave. After what happened on this trip, I doubt I'll ever be brave."

"You did fine, especially considering what we ran into. And I have to say, the amount of care you showed those poor people on the trip back was amazing. I don't know that I would've had the patience."

"I like helping people. It's why I became a healer. It's fighting I have trouble with."

It took about an hour to reach the main gate. Danny let Edith take the lead. He'd noticed that priests of Adonael got a lot of respect. May as well use that to their advantage.

"How can we help you, Priestess?" the lead guard asked.

"I have important business at the temple. If you could let us in, I would be most grateful."

"And this fellow with you?"

"My bodyguard."

Danny took out his guild badge. "I'm Ronin, journeyman adventurer."

"Right." The guard made a motion with his hand and the portcullis started up. "In you get."

"Oh," Edith said before they entered. "Our friends will be coming along with some wagons. They've got injured people and will be keeping their distance from the city. They're not a threat, but I wanted to let you know."

Danny ushered her through before the guards had a chance to ask questions.

He let Edith stay in the lead as they strode down the main road through the city. Danny hadn't spent much time exploring Rosenbar and had no idea where the temples might be. Edith strode ahead without hesitation which made him feel better.

"Did you train to be a priestess at this temple?" Danny asked.

"Yes. Adonael called me to her service when I turned thirteen. It took four years to finish my training, then I served as an initiate for a year, healing the sick and injured, and generally doing what the older priests told me to, until I felt the call to adventure. What about you?"

"What do you mean?"

"Why did you become an adventurer?"

"It seemed like a good way to use my skills to make money. I never cared much for serving the nobility, so joining the army was out. That left mercenary or adventurer. I generally prefer working alone, so I chose the latter. I'll be honest, I didn't think my first adventure would turn out quite like this."

"Me either. Rescuing villagers is a far cry from fetching vegetables. I think it's a miracle no one got hurt despite everything we went through."

Danny smiled. He didn't consider his efforts miraculous, but he'd done his best to keep everyone safe.

Edith turned off the main road and into a section of the city filled with towering structures, five of them in fact. All were made of stone of a similar style but featuring unique details that differentiated them.

"This is the temple district," Edith said when she noticed him looking around. "The five most worshipped archangels have temples here. Adonael's is the largest and most elaborate as is befitting her status as the savior of Valindor."

"Who are the others?" Danny asked.

"The Goddess, Lady of Healing; Branik the Sword Lord; the Queen of Coins; and the Binder in Chains." She gave a little shiver at the last one.

"Is the Binder not popular?"

"No, he is, but it's a very strict faith. His priests are very rigid in applying what they consider divine law. Luckily the other temples don't put up with their nonsense and the trouble they cause is kept to a minimum. Here we are."

Edith paused in front of a white stone temple that had the same basic design as the Crystal Cathedral. A golden circle over the door marked it as Adonael's temple.

"Should I wait out here?" Danny asked.

"Don't be silly. All are welcome in Adonael's house."

Edith strode up the steps and pushed through the unlocked doors. As he expected, there were rows of pews facing an altar draped with white cloth. A woman dressed in familiar white-and-gold robes emerged from a door built into the rear wall. Danny guessed her age at midforties. Her dark hair had streaks of gray running through it and fine lines surrounded her eyes. She offered them a gentle, warm smile.

"Sister Edith. I hadn't expected you to return to us so soon. And you've brought a friend." That last bit was as much a question as a statement.

"Ronin is a member of my team. We've run into a serious problem, Sister Mary." Edith told her everything that happened. "The others will be in position soon. Can the temple help?"

"Of course. It's our duty despite so many of our brothers and sisters being out of the city, fighting." Sister Mary turned to Danny. "You're sure it's magical compulsion keeping them as they are and not illness?"

"Whether they're ill or not I can't say, but I am certain someone embedded a spell in their brains. I can see it as plain as day. What I can't do, at least I'm not confident I can, is safely remove it. I thought it would be best to leave that to people with more experience."

"A very wise decision. You could actually do more damage to the victim removing the spell than the original caster did activating it in the first place. I'll send someone to alert the other temples. This is a bigger task than we can handle on our own."

"Excuse the interruption, but would one of you be Ronin?" Danny shifted so he could look past Sister Mary. Standing in the doorway was a woman that appeared to be easily in her nineties. She was bent over and thin, her face a mass of wrinkles. But her blue eyes were bright and alert. There was no sign of mental decline in them.

"Mother Superior." Sister Mary bowed and Edith quickly did the same. "Did you need something?"

"A moment of this young man's time." Her intense gaze never wavered from Danny.

He wasn't sure he wanted to hear whatever she had to say. Only a higher power could have told her Danny's new name. What else the archangel might have told her was what worried him.

He was about to beg off when Edith said, "Don't keep her waiting. We can handle things from here on."

Danny swallowed a sigh. No way was he getting out of it now. "Sure. Where should we talk?"

"My office is in the back," the Mother Superior said. "This way. I can make us tea. Do you like tea?"

Danny had no strong feelings about tea one way or the other. "Tea's fine, thank you."

The old woman led him deeper into the church. Every so often the walls would be decorated with a painting of a woman dressed in priestly vestments. The last one at the end of the hall looked like Eve. Were they paintings of the priestesses chosen to summon the other heroes? It seemed likely but Danny wasn't about to point out that he recognized Eve.

Behind a closed door was a small, cozy office that more closely resembled a sitting room than a place of business. Four comfortable-looking leather chairs surrounded a low coffee table while a bookcase filled with leather-bound tomes ran along the back wall.

"Have a seat and make yourself comfortable. I can tell you're nervous. Rest assured you're in no danger from me."

Danny was less worried about her than he was her boss. Still, there was no getting away now. He sat in the nearest chair. The ether stirred as she conjured tea into fine porcelain cups. She set one in front of Danny then sat across from him. The moment her butt hit the cushion her blue eyes turned golden and began to glow.

"Hero." A new voice spoke from the old woman's mouth. "Your work is not complete. The demon king survived and is even now gathering her strength. You must hunt her down and finish your task."

"Adonael, I assume? That's not happening. I have a new mission. You'll have to find someone else to take this one on. If there's nothing else, I need to go."

"You cannot abandon the quest. The hero's duty is clear and you must fulfill it."

Danny shook his head. "Didn't you hear? The hero's dead.

132

It was announced all over the kingdom. I've died twice for your stupid game. I'm not going to die for it a third time."

Her eyes blazed brighter and the room shook. "Would you make an enemy of an archangel? I have thousands, tens of thousands of followers. They will hound you to the ends of Valindor."

Danny shook his head. It was an empty threat and they both knew it. "No offense, but you've got enough problems without siccing your followers on someone that's not causing you any trouble. And don't think just because I'm a nice guy that I'll go down easy. Someone tries to kill me then you'd better believe I'll return the favor. Death and I are well acquainted."

The glow dimmed and the vibrations stopped. When Adonael spoke again, she sounded incredibly tired. "If you fail in this task, the world is doomed to millennia of darkness. I understand your anger. It's justified. But would you abandon the entire population for the act of one person?"

"This isn't my world. As a soldier of Earth, my duty is to protect the people of my home world. If I can help a few people here in the process, I'm okay with that, but I refuse to fail in the most important mission. No more innocents will die for your game."

"You mean to destroy the ritual circle." Adonael shook her head. "It's impossible. The half-elves created a spell of such power and perfection even Heaven was awed. Your power, great though it might be, is insufficient to break it."

Danny shrugged. "We'll see. Can I go now? I can't imagine housing your spirit is healthy for that old lady."

"I would never harm one of my followers. Go then, and think on what I said. Think about the innocent people who will suffer for your inaction."

The glow faded and when it did, old-lady snores filled the room. Looked like she'd be okay. He spotted a blanket folded up beside the bookcase, grabbed it, and tucked her in. Hopefully she'd get a nice nap.

Danny slipped out of the room and retraced his steps. Somehow he doubted this would be the last he heard from Adonael.

CHAPTER 17

Lyra strode through the streets of Rosenbar. After her failure at the demon church she found herself depressed. She didn't know what to do next. That was rare for her. There was always another move to make, but think as she might, Lyra didn't know what it might be.

Beside her, Eve was staring at the cobblestones. She'd taken their failure nearly as hard as Lyra herself. It wasn't her fault. Unless the tip of the mithril sword could penetrate the portal, her divine power couldn't seal it. The failure was Lyra's and no one else's.

Speaking of no one else, she'd left their squad of knights back at the inn. The human knights had proven a remarkable disappointment. She swallowed a sigh. That wasn't fair, but it was also the truth. Daniel could've beaten the lot of them without batting an eye.

Lyra stopped and frowned as a dozen people dressed in the vestments of multiple faiths came running toward them. The priests and priestesses were clearly in a hurry to get somewhere. She'd heard no alarm bells and saw no panic in the streets. What the hell could be happening?

"Excuse me." Eve grabbed the arm of a passing priest of Adonael. "What's going on?"

The young man took one look at her and his jaw dropped. "High Priestess Carre, I didn't know you were in the city. Adonael must be looking out for us. Adventurers just brought scores of people back from an outlying village. They've been ensorcelled by demons. All the city's priests are going to try and help them. Your skill would be most welcome."

Eve nodded and let him go. She turned to Lyra. "I have to help if I can."

"Go then. Perhaps something good can come from this debacle. I'd join you but I know my presence is more likely to distract the rest of the priests than to help. I'll meet you at the inn tonight."

Eve looked like she wanted to argue, but in the end they both knew the truth. With a little sigh, Eve trotted off after the rest of the priests. Lyra watched until she was out of sight then trudged on. She had no destination in mind; she just found her thinking clearer when she was moving.

It was a considerable shock when, a block later, she sensed familiar magic. Homing in on it, she soon spotted Daniel. He'd shaved his head and grown a beard, but it was definitely him. The magic she sensed came from his ring. Likely no one else would've recognized it, but since she helped him make it, she'd never mistake it for anything else. Lyra would've bet the royal treasury he was one of the adventurers who rescued those villagers from the demons.

In fact, given the power of the average human, she could almost guarantee it.

Lyra had no doubt her presence would not be welcome to him, but she had to try and convince him to help her. Sealing those portals was something only he could do.

Once she made up her mind, Lyra hurried to catch up with him. When she was ten strides away he stopped and turned to face her. His grim scowl confirmed her theory. Daniel was not happy to see her.

"What are you, some kind of stalker?" he asked. "Did I not make my desire to never see you again clear?"

"You made it clear, but some things have happened. Perhaps you noticed?"

"Yeah. What do you want?"

"I thought we might compare notes, then I have a proposal."

"I don't like the sound of any of that, but given the results of my last job, it might be a good idea. I'm supposed to meet the rest of the team tonight, but I've got a couple hours. Talking in the street might not be the best idea. Any other suggestions?"

"Eve and I, along with a small group of arcane knights, are staying at an inn not far from here. We can talk in my room."

"Fine, lead on."

Lyra was disappointed but hardly surprised with Daniel's reaction. His willingness to speak with her in greater detail was a victory as far as she was concerned. Whether anything else came of it, time would tell.

○

Danny had never been blessed with the best luck. If he'd had any doubt about that, running into Lyra after getting a lecture from Adonael herself confirmed it. His first thought was to ignore her, but trading information was valuable enough that he decided to put his distaste aside and listen.

And now here he was, in her modest room, seated across from her at a small, round table. It was so much like his conversation with Adonael that he wondered if fate had a sense of humor.

Lyra leaned forward. "Thank you for agreeing to speak with me. I know you have no reason to oblige me even that much."

"True. So, you want to go first or should I?"

"I will. I had a theory that the churches were still active and bringing in more monsters and demons. Given our limited success so far, it seemed reasonable. Eve and I set out with the knights to find out for sure. We went to a church not far from here, the next one in line from the two you sealed. When we arrived, the portal was inactive and we found no guards and no priestess. Despite my best efforts, I wasn't strong enough to pierce the portal so Eve could seal it. I fear only you are."

"I can tell you where the priestess went: the village my team and I visited." Danny filled her in on the events of the past few days. "She was there with a succubus and had all the villagers under her thumb. Best I can tell, they're using the post-invasion chaos to imbed sleeper cells in Villipan. And if they're doing it here, you can bet they're doing it elsewhere. Not sure if they've moved into the bigger cities yet, but we didn't want anyone taking control of the villagers again, so we stopped outside the walls."

"That was a wise decision. I've never heard the phrase sleeper cell before, but I can guess what it means. I swear, the more I hear about this demon king's plan, the more I fear her. Clearly we're dealing with someone far more clever than any we've faced."

"How do you plan to deal with it?" Danny asked.

"I'll let Richard know what we've learned, with no mention being made of you and your survival of course. Teams of wizards and knights can root out any demons that might be making a home where they're not wanted. It will be time consuming, but most things worth doing are. I still think the portals need to be sealed. We don't want to make it easy for the demon king to summon reinforcements when she returns. Assuming you're still determined not to hunt her down."

"You sound like Adonael. No, I'm not going to act as your hunting dog."

"What do you mean I sound like Adonael?"

Danny told her about his conversation with the archangel. "I don't know what it is with you people, but convincing someone you've murdered to help solve your problems isn't likely to happen. As soon as things are calm enough and I've completed my ten missions to achieve elite rank, I mean to leave for Elfhome. After that, the Five Kingdoms are on their own."

"Why would you want to go to that corrupted, demon-haunted place?"

"I figure I can find more details about the summoning ritual. I don't care what Adonael says, there has to be some way to destroy it."

"Two rounds remain in the great game," Lyra said. "If you destroy the ritual, I don't know what the demon lords might do. It's possible they might call it off. All the sacrifices the other heroes made would be for nothing."

Danny shrugged. "I can do nothing for the dead. Right now my focus is on making sure no other innocents from my world end up murdered for your cause. That is my right and proper responsibility."

He watched Lyra's face twist and grimace as she thought. At last her expression smoothed and she said, "So be it. Will you help me seal the portals?"

Now it was Danny's turn to hesitate. Much as he didn't want anything more to do with her, this could work out to his advantage, assuming he played his cards right.

"I have conditions."

"Name them. If they're within my power, consider them granted."

"One, you go through the guild. Post a job for a scout to go into Fell Forest. That will be more than enough to convince no one else to take it and if it isn't, your name will finish the job. And I want a hundred small gold pieces per portal."

"Agreed. What else?"

He wanted to make her promise to not kill any more of the heroes, but doubted she'd hesitate to break her word when the time came. It wasn't like someone willing to murder would care about breaking an oath.

Instead he said, "You tell Eve the truth, all of it. I want to be there when you do."

Lyra grimaced. "She wears her emotions as openly as her clothes. If we tell her everything, I doubt she'll be able to hide it when she sees Richard again. It might give your survival away."

"I'll take my chances. Besides, as soon as we reach the first portal, she'll know who I am anyway. And you know she'll have questions. Better to get everything out in the open up front."

"Fine, anything else?"

"Two things. Get rid of the knights. They'll only slow us down. And finally, I'm still under contract with Trevor. We need to bring supplies into the city. I can't help you until I finish that."

"I think my task is a little more important."

Danny shook his head. Of course she thought that. "It's my first guild contract. How's it going to look if I dump it and move on? Unlike you, I need to build a positive reputation. By the way, my new name is Ronin. Call me by it whenever we're in public."

Lyra finally smiled. "A warrior without a master, it suits you."

"I figured one of the other heroes would've mentioned the word to you at some point." Danny stood. "I'm supposed to meet the rest of the team at Trevor's warehouse so we can make plans for the next run. I'll be back tonight to talk to you and Eve."

"I appreciate you doing this. I'm aware you have no reason to help me."

Danny headed for the door. "I've decided to treat your request like I would any other potential job. If I think of it as doing something dangerous for money, it doesn't turn my stomach so badly. Until later."

He stepped out into the hall and closed the door behind him. What was he thinking? Danny couldn't believe he'd agreed to help her again. One thing was for sure, he wasn't going to let her get behind him.

CHAPTER 18

His walk back to the warehouse was a quiet one. Danny suspected that most of the city's attention was focused on what was going on outside the walls. He hoped the priests could help those people. Seeing them lying around like still-breathing corpses sickened him. It was wrong on so many levels. Despite his change in plans, he had no intention of letting the demons do whatever they wanted with these people. Danny would happily destroy them whenever he stumbled across one.

He turned down the street that led to Trevor's warehouse. Robi was standing outside and waved as Danny approached. "Thought you got lost."

"I ran into an old friend on my way and we stopped to chat. I'm meeting her for dinner later, but I wanted to come by and see what the plan was for our next run."

"Ooh, a lady friend, is it? You'll have to tell me about it tomorrow. Everyone else is inside. Now that you're back, we can start the meeting."

Danny nodded and followed him inside. He saw no point

correcting his mistake about Lyra. Let Robi imagine what-ever he wanted. It would certainly be better than the truth.

Everyone was standing around on the far side of the warehouse. Given the size of Trevor's office, it made more sense to have the meeting out here.

As they approached, Danny waved. "Sorry to hold you all up. Where are the wagons?"

"Still outside the city," Martin said. "The priest I spoke to said they'd need them for the rest of the day and maybe longer. Did you know the high priestess of Adonael's church was in the city visiting? Talk about a lucky break."

"That is lucky," Danny said. "So what's the plan?"

"As soon as we get our wagons back," Trevor said. "You all are going back to collect those crops. It should be simple given that all the demons and monsters between here and the village have been killed."

"Uh, that's not really how it works," Danny said. "It's not like there's a wall and once you kill all the demons inside, you're finished. More can come in at any time. Assuming otherwise is a good way to end up dead."

Trevor looked pained. "Of course, I know that. But surely there must be some limit to how many of the cursed things are in the kingdom. Can't they torment some other area?"

"I'm sure plenty of other places are being tormented," Danny said.

"I'm expressing myself poorly today." Trevor scrubbed a hand across his bald head. "I wish ill on no one, I'm just so frustrated. We need to get those supplies in and the sooner the better. With the farmers out of commission, I don't know if we'll even have a fall harvest."

"We'll do our best, sir," Robi said. "If there's no one at the farms to pay, will it be okay for us to take the crops?"

"Luis already paid the farmers, so that's no problem," Trevor said. "Will your team be ready to head out tomorrow?"

"We'll be ready, assuming the priests return our wagons by then." Robi scratched the stubble on his cheek. "Given how many people we brought back, they might not be finished by morning."

The rest of the team offered murmurs of agreement.

Danny had no idea how long it might take to dispel that many spells, but with Eve helping, he hoped it wouldn't be too long.

"Did you need anything else?" Danny asked.

"No," Trevor said. "I guess that's all. Hardly seems like we even needed a meeting. Still, it's good to confirm you're all still committed, especially you, Ronin, since you're a contract hire. You technically made the trip and got the wagons back safely. You're within your rights to claim the contract is complete."

Danny cocked his head. "What kind of piss-poor excuse for an adventurer would do that? I was hired to escort supplies. The fact that we ended up rescuing some villagers instead doesn't change the job. This is my first guild contract and I mean to see it through properly."

Robi clapped him on the shoulder. "That's the way a real adventurer talks. I knew we could count on you."

The others agreed and took turns shaking his hand.

Edith went last and said, "I'll feel a lot safer with you joining us."

Danny grinned back. "I'll do my best. Guild Master Duret said I should get my elite badge before I leave the Five King-doms and I plan to follow his advice."

"You're leaving?" Trevor asked. "To go where?"

"West to begin with. I want to see the world. My first goal is to visit Elfhome. I bet I can find all kinds of magical treasures hidden in the ruins."

"What's Elfhome?" Bertram asked.

"The ancient homeland of the elf-bloods," Danny said. "It was their capital when they ruled the continent."

Bertram shrugged. "Never heard of it."

"If you're planning to travel," Trevor said. "Perhaps you'd like to join my son when he leaves on a grand caravan. I'd feel better knowing you were there to scout for him."

Now it was Danny's turn to be confused. His host's memories didn't mention the word. "What's that?"

"A huge caravan that travels the world trading with many lands. They're sometimes gone for decades." Trevor offered a wistful smile. "I never went on one myself, so I'm quite jealous that my son is getting the chance. He's been saving money and trade goods for five years in preparation. He'll likely return a rich man. He planned to leave this summer, but it's still too dangerous to pass through Fell Forest, even if they keep to the trade road. Hopefully he can leave in the fall. If he turns south he can trade through the winter before heading back north in the spring."

"Sounds like you want to go with him," Robi said.

Trevor chuckled. "Don't I wish? But I'm too old for something like that. I'd likely die on the road, a prospect which doesn't appeal to me. No, a grand caravan is a young man's game."

"As long as they're heading in the same direction I am, then I'd be happy to lend a hand," Danny said. "But I wouldn't take a contract, since I may need to go my own way eventually."

"That's perfectly fair," Trevor said. "I'll mention it to my son and introduce you sometime. Are we all agreed that you'll head out again as soon as the wagons are returned?"

Robi nodded. "We'll be ready, sir."

"I have plans for tonight," Danny said. "But I'll be back in the morning. Until then."

"Don't do anything I wouldn't do," Robi said.

Danny grinned, perfectly willing to play along. "What don't you do?"

Melia laughed. "He doesn't do anything. If he did, his wife would kill him."

Robi managed to look pained. "She's not wrong. See you in the morning."

"Right." Danny waved and headed for the exit. As he walked, he tried to figure out why Robi didn't live with his wife instead of staying at the barracks, but finally decided it was none of his business.

Theorizing did take his mind off the coming conversation with Eve and that was welcome. Somehow he doubted tonight was going to be pleasant.

CHAPTER 19

Eve had been tired before. Many times before, in fact, but never as tired as she was now. The sun had long since set and her weary eyes could barely focus on the details of the street. Only the gentle hand of the youthful priest of Adonael guiding her kept Eve on the right path. They'd offered her a room at the temple, but she very much preferred to stay in her room at the inn. Her coreligionists tended to fuss more than Eve liked. It came with being the chosen high priestess of Adonael.

The priests had succeeded in freeing all the villagers of the demons' magic, though it had taken all they had. The people were still unconscious, alas, but when they woke, their minds would be their own. It always felt good to use her power to help people. Even if it did leave her an exhausted mess.

"This is your inn, High Priestess," the young man said. "It was a great honor to watch you work today. I'll never forget it."

"Just happy to help," Eve said through a yawn.

"I'll take her from here." Lady Shael stepped out of the shadows cast by the inn.

"Yes, ma'am." The priest fled as if expecting to get devoured.

Eve giggled. She might not like being fussed over, but she didn't know how Lady Shael stood everyone being afraid of her. Not that their reactions seemed to bother her much. Maybe the key was not caring what people thought about you.

"Have you been waiting for me?" Eve asked.

"I have." Lady Shael took her gently by the elbow and guided her toward the inn's door. "Something important has happened and we need to talk about it at once."

"I'm too tired to think, much less talk. Won't it keep until morning?"

"It will not. I believe I've found a solution to our portal problem."

Eve perked up a bit. "Really? How? I haven't been gone that long."

"The answer is waiting upstairs." Lady Shael guided her through the front door, across the common room, and up the steps.

Eve was vaguely aware of people watching them, but no one spoke. That was fine as she had nothing to say. It was taking every bit of focus she had to put one foot in front of the other. At the top of the stairs they turned toward Lady Shael's room.

When the door opened, she stared in confusion. An unfamiliar man sat in one of the room's two chairs. Did she know anyone with a bald head and beard? Didn't seem like it. Long hair was more common in Villipan, especially among the people she dealt with regularly.

"Hello, Eve." The man's familiar voice sent a lightning bolt through her, fully washing away all her fatigue. It simply wasn't possible.

"Daniel?"

"That's right. I didn't expect us to meet again, but some things happened and here we are. It's good to see you."

"How? We buried you."

"Tell her, Lyra. Tell her all of it."

Eve dragged her gaze away from Daniel. "What's he talking about?"

"I'm going to tell you the truth," Lady Shael said. "It's an ugly truth, but the truth all the same. Please ask no questions until I'm finished."

Eve nodded, thoroughly confused.

Lady Shael told her everything, how she killed Daniel and the other heroes at the kings' command. She didn't seem upset about her crimes. If Eve had murdered five people she wouldn't have been able to live with herself. Maybe it was an elf-blood thing. It's not like she was killing one of her own kind.

When she finished, Eve wasn't sure exactly what to say. "Are you telling me King Richard ordered you to kill Daniel because he didn't want to pay to have him live in the mansion? That sounds insane."

"It's not so simple. After Toshiro defeated the first demon king, the ruler of Villipan at the time demanded an oath of loyalty from him. Toshiro refused. He said he served the people, not the king."

"Bet that went over well," Daniel said.

"It went exactly as you'd expect. No king wants his decrees questioned, much less by someone who commands the people's loyalty. Had he wished it, Toshiro could've led the commoners in an uprising and taken over the country. He was an honorable young man and wouldn't have done so without grave cause, but the potential remained, hanging over the king's head. The story was passed from father to son, king to prince. When the second cycle began, it was made clear to me that if the hero survived the battle with the demon king, I was to make sure he didn't make it out of the castle. With my people's safety on the line, I had no choice but to obey."

"If you killed Daniel—and he certainly looked dead to me —how is he still alive?"

"Dumb luck," Daniel said. "After I freed the drake from his slave collar, he was kind enough to offer me two items as a reward, an ethersword and a star ring. I used the star ring's wish to resurrect myself. I'm not sure why it triggered after you buried me, probably some mistake in my wording. Anyway, that's why I'm back among the living."

"That's… a lot to take in. Whatever the circumstances, I'm glad you're alive. May I further assume you're the solution to our portal problem?"

He nodded. "I agreed to help but only if Lyra went through the guild. I'll take a separate contract for each portal. I help you close them and you help me fund my journey."

Eve offered an enthusiastic nod. "Your journey to hunt down the demon king. The temple will be happy to provide resources as well."

"No, not to hunt down the demon king. I'm going to destroy the spell that allows you to summon people from my world."

That couldn't be right. "You can't. If we lose the ability to summon a hero, we'll have no chance against the next demon king."

Daniel shrugged. "Not my problem. My duty is to my own world, not yours. No more innocent people will die if I can help it."

His cold, hard expression made it clear he meant every word. And Eve couldn't blame him. After the way he'd been treated, it was ridiculous to imagine he'd have any loyalty toward Villipan. They were lucky he was willing to help close the portals.

"I assume we're heading back out tomorrow," Eve said.

"No," Daniel said. "I've still got a contract to finish. I'll be leaving with Robi's team to collect the harvest and bring it back for storage. Once that's done and I register the completed contract, I'll take yours. Best guess, early next week."

"What are we supposed to do until then?" Eve asked.

Daniel stood and shrugged again. "Whatever you like. I'm not overly interested. I'll meet you here after I get your contract. Good evening."

And with that he walked out the door.

Eve turned to Lady Shael. She wasn't sure what to think about the elf-blood woman now. But regardless, they had work to do and she couldn't let her feelings get in the way.

"To answer your question, we're going to the capital to talk to Richard. I'm sure I don't need to tell you this, but not a word about what we just discussed to him."

"Of course," Eve said. "Daniel seems very upset."

Lady Shael's smile was humorless. "You're a shrewd observer of the human condition."

Eve's cheeks warmed. That had been a stupid thing to say and she deserved the sarcasm. Shock and exhaustion had her brain scrambled.

"Do you think he can destroy the summoning spell?"

Lady Shael let out a long, exhausted-sounding sigh. "I don't know. It's doubtful given the scope of it, but breaking things is a lot easier than making them, so maybe. And maybe that's a good thing. Instead of hiding behind summoned heroes, we'll have to figure out a way to win our own battles."

Eve rubbed her tired eyes. That was nice to say, but if it were possible, Adonael wouldn't have taught them how to summon a hero in the first place.

CHAPTER 20

Four days of hard riding brought Lyra, Eve, and the knights back to Villipan City. Thankfully everything looked peaceful. If an emergency had befallen the capital, on top of all the other problems they had at the moment, Lyra wasn't sure what she would've done. Speaking to Richard would be treacherous enough.

The gate guards waved them through without issue and they guided their mounts toward the castle. The streets were busy and the people seemed relaxed and content. Must be nice.

When they reached the turnoff to the castle Eve said, "I'll be at the cathedral preparing. When you're ready to return, come get me."

Lyra nodded. The story they concocted was that Eve would be praying to Adonael for the power to seal the portals. It would provide both an excuse for her not appearing before the king and for them returning and, with Daniel's help, successfully sealing the portals. The story was mainly for the knights. She knew how soldiers gossiped.

Better they spread the story she wanted spread than one of simple failure.

"We should be good to leave tomorrow. I hope your prayers bear fruit."

Lyra and the knights turned toward the castle while Eve guided her mount down the street to the cathedral. This really was for the best. Eve might've been the worst liar Lyra had ever met. As soon as she was in Richard's presence he would've been certain to notice something was off.

The guards on duty asked them a couple standard questions before letting them through. In the courtyard the leader of the arcane knights said, "If there's nothing else, Lady Shael, we'll head for the barracks."

"By all means. And thank you for your assistance."

"We did little enough, but if it was of some use, then we were happy to do so. Good morning."

The knights left her and she was on her own again. That was for the best too. Lyra generally operated at her peak when no one was holding her back. The only problem was, her peak often didn't reach high enough to solve her problems.

Using her magic to guide her, Lyra strode through the castle at a pace that told the servants to get out of her way and not to bother her. Basically, it was how she always walked through the castle.

She found the king in the war room. She knocked twice on the closed door and a moment later a muffled voice said, "Go away."

"It's Lyra. I have a new report."

A moment later the door opened and Richard looked at her with dark, bloodshot eyes. If he'd been getting more than a few hours' sleep a night she would've been surprised. Not that his sleep habits interested Lyra overly much, but exhaustion tended to lead to poor reasoning and she needed Richard sharp enough to lead the humans through the current crisis.

"Please tell me you have good news." He sounded so desperate it was pathetic.

"No, I don't have good news." She told him about the dominated villagers. "You're going to need to have wizards and knights search for infiltrators."

"I don't have any spare wizards or knights. Everyone is busy hunting demons all over the countryside. They are making progress, thank Adonael, but if I pull any of our magic users out of the field, the effort will falter. Only their magic allows the warriors to have a chance against the demons. Do you understand? The army is stretched tighter than a bowstring. One more thing and they'll snap."

"I understand perfectly," Lyra said. "You must do what you think is best for the kingdom. I'm simply providing you with the best information I can. Did you request the temples deploy some of the priests from Rosenbar? Also, Eve and I will be heading back out tomorrow. Our first effort to close the portal was a failure, but she thinks she's found a way to remedy that, assuming Adonael answers her prayers."

"I wish the archangel would answer mine. I hope Eve has better luck. As for the priests, I put in a request with the temples, so we'll see. Come in for a moment. I'd like you to show me on the map where the village was found."

She slipped past him and went over to the map table. It looked like a pincushion. She marked the village with a red pin since all the black ones were in use. "Right there. It's a piddling little place of no strategic importance. Nothing but farmers and a few tradesmen. According to the adventurers that rescued them, every villager was under the control of the priestess."

"It's a miracle they didn't end up added to that number. These adventurers must be highly skilled."

Lyra needed to steer the conversation in another direction, quickly. "They were lucky. One of them took the priestess by surprise and dealt a fatal blow. It could easily have gone the other way. Has King Miles and his family made themselves at home?"

Richard rubbed his face and slumped into a handy chair. "They were in rough shape when they arrived. Sounds like the attack pretty much destroyed their capital city. I can't imagine how many deaths that would be. I pray nightly it doesn't happen here and then I have nightmares that it will."

A bitter, angry part of Lyra almost hoped it did. Almost. In the end, her fate was tied to Villipan's. Anything that was bad for the kingdom was bad for her and her people.

"Forte is the smallest of the Five Kingdoms. It would take a much larger effort to crush Villipan City."

"I know, I know. And we have plans to flee to the cathedral should the worst happen. But knowing it and believing it are two different things. The worst part is that I can't even send the prince and princesses to safety when nowhere is safe."

Lyra had no idea what he wanted her to say so she nodded. "It's a difficult situation. One we can hopefully learn from for the next cycle. Not that I imagine the next demon king will use the same tactics."

"By the archangels I hope not. One big battle and that's the end of it is so much better than this chaos."

Easy for him to say since he wouldn't be the one doing

the fighting. "I need to make some preparations before Eve and I leave again in the morning."

"Yes, fine, I'm just rambling. I have to keep up appearances for everyone, but somehow I feel I can be honest with you. I wonder why you inspire such confidence in me."

"My loyal service to the throne of Villipan for over a thousand years probably has something to do with it. Stay strong, Richard. Your people need you." She wanted to spit to get the bad taste of those words out of her mouth.

"I'll do the best I can. Should you succeed in dealing with the portals, that will be a weight off my mind."

She bowed and withdrew, unwilling to make promises she couldn't keep. Even with Daniel's help, she had no guarantee they would succeed.

Eve let out a soft sigh as she entered the Crystal Cathedral. It was a homecoming of sorts. While she wasn't born here, she had spent almost as much of her life in the cathedral as she did in the village of her birth.

The pews were empty as usual. People seldom came to visit save on Holy Day. Eve always thought that was a shame. You could pray to Adonael any time you wanted, not just one day a week. Part of her liked to think they were praying at home, but the rest of her knew the truth. People were too busy to take the time.

Understandable of course. Life wasn't as easy for the average person as it had been for her.

She walked down the central aisle toward the altar. The white covering was a little off center. Not a big deal, but if someone should show up, she wanted everything to look as perfect as possible. As soon as she touched the cloth a white light filled her vision and she was once again floating among the clouds of Heaven.

A moment later, Adonael's perfect form appeared before her. "You have made contact with the hero."

It wasn't really a question, but Eve answered anyway. "I have. I can't believe Daniel is still alive."

"I would call it a divine miracle, but I played no part in making it happen. I can play no part in what must happen next, either."

Eve cocked her head. "What must happen next?"

"You must convince him to hunt down and finish off the demon king rather than waste his time attempting to destroy the summoning spell. He's doomed to failure in the latter, but he can do some good with the former."

Eve swallowed hard. They hadn't spoken for long, but Daniel made it pretty clear he had no intention of doing anything of the sort. She couldn't exactly say that to her patron. When the archangel you worshipped gave you a task, there was only one thing you could say.

"I'll do my best."

"You must succeed. However bad you imagine things might get should the demon king win, it will, in fact, be far worse. All the world's hopes ride on your shoulders, my chosen. Do whatever you must, but do not fail."

A hand touched her shoulder and when Eve turned her head she saw the kind but worried face of Sister Rose right beside her.

"Are you okay?" Sister Rose asked.

"Yes, fine. The altar cover was slightly askew and I

thought I'd straighten it before I returned to my room. Has all been calm while I was away?"

"Of course. You haven't been away for that long. The people were disappointed when you weren't here to lead the Holy Day prayer, but that was the biggest thing to happen." Sister Rose frowned, the little wrinkle between her brows getting deeper as she thought. "Actually, that's not true. The arrival of King Miles was the biggest thing. People seldom get to see a foreign king. The royal family looked a bit rough."

She said that last sentence in a low voice as if someone might overhear her and take offense. Eve knew what the family had been through and figured if the worst thing that happened was a haggard look, then they got out of it easy.

"It was a long trip back and I'm exhausted. I think I'll take a nap." Eve took a step toward the door that led to her room.

"Are you back for good?" Sister Rose asked.

Eve offered a wan smile. "No, I'll be leaving tomorrow with Lady Shael. Our mission has only begun and I fear it will get harder before the end."

"Well, don't forget to take care of yourself as well. The faith needs its high priestess."

She nodded and trudged on toward the back of the cathedral. Lady Shael needed her to seal the portals, Adonael needed her to convince Daniel to complete the hero's mission, and the faith needed her for… some unspecified reason. It seemed everyone needed her.

Except Daniel, who only needed to be left alone. Pity she wasn't going to be able to grant his wish.

CHAPTER 21

Danny's second trip out to the demon-haunted village with Robi's team was a piece of cake. They didn't encounter a single demon or monster the entire way out or back. It was like after killing the priestess and rescuing the villagers, all the evil things in the area split. That was fine with Danny. After everything they dealt with on the first trip, he figured they deserved an easy run. Especially since they brought four wagons with them this time.

All four wagons were now loaded with a variety of vegetables with squash predominating. As they rolled down the street toward Trevor's warehouse, Danny yawned and stretched. He'd completed his first job as an adventurer and then some. He imagined it would've felt like a bigger deal, but compared to some of the things he'd done, it just seemed ordinary. But, ordinary or not, the gold would be most welcome.

When they rounded the corner, they found the warehouse doors open and workers waiting to unload the wagons. Trevor stood off to one side, a big smile on his face.

That was a nice change. Up until now all Danny had seen was the worried frown and the tired frown.

He jumped off and walked over to the merchant and soon the rest of the team joined him.

"Mission accomplished," Robi said. "We didn't even have to fight once. It was a welcome change."

Trevor clapped once. "Well done, all of you. It's only a start, but this load of supplies will make a big difference when winter arrives. Take a couple days to recover and we'll start planning the next trip."

Danny pulled the contract out of his satchel. "About that. I've got another job lined up, so I'll have to pass."

Trevor's smile withered. "Are you certain? I might be able to up the reward to ten small gold pieces. I could even take you on as a permanent member of the team."

"That's very generous of you, but as I said, I plan to leave the Five Kingdoms as soon as I reach elite status. A friend of mine turned me on to a job that pays well and will allow me to explore more of the other kingdoms. It's too good of an opportunity to pass up. Given our recent trip, I feel confident the worst of the trouble in this area has passed. Robi and the others should be fine."

"I won't deny my disappointment," Trevor said. "But you did help us a great deal and you lived up to your contract. No one can ask more than that from an adventurer. Come to my office and I'll sign it."

The brief walk didn't take long and soon enough Danny was back in the warehouse.

He shook hands with Robi. "It's been interesting. Good luck on your next trip."

"Same to you in your new job. I can't deny we'll miss you

on the next one. If you change your mind, there will always be a place for you on my team."

"Hear, hear!" Bertram said.

Another round of handshakes and goodbyes and Danny was off to the guild. Lyra should've posted her contract by now. He didn't want to hang around wasting his money on a room at an inn. The sooner they got started, the sooner they'd finish.

Walking through the streets, a few people glanced his way, but no one spoke. He was one of the few armed people out and about. In fact, the only other people he'd seen with weapons were a pair of guards with iron truncheons hanging at their belt. Danny offered them a polite nod and got the same in return. Just like the MPs on base, they wouldn't bother you if you didn't cause trouble.

At last he reached the guild and strode through the door. As with his first arrival, the waiting area was full, largely, he assumed, with the same people as before. He spotted Bruno seated at the very same table. This time he didn't try to block Danny from reaching the counter.

Emily smiled as he approached. "Welcome back. I was worried you might run into trouble, but it seems everything worked out okay."

Danny grinned and placed the signed contract on the counter. "You could say that, though it ended up being a bigger job than I expected. You heard about the villagers we brought back?"

"Everyone in Rosenbar did. You'll have to tell me the whole story sometime." The way she looked at him when she said it made Danny wonder if leaving quickly was the best idea after all. "The contract looks good. I'll get your coins."

She went down to the far end of the counter and

crouched. The clink of coins followed and then she straightened, a little cloth bag in her hand. "Here you go."

He hefted the bag and frowned. "This feels like too much."

"There's a bonus. Trevor came in a couple days ago to arrange it. He said you deserved something for going well beyond the contract requirements. I also made a note on your guild record that you completed your first job."

"Thanks. When I move on to another guild, how do they know where I am as far as rank?"

"That's easy. If you're planning to leave the Rosenbar guild's area of activity, just let me know and I'll prepare a letter for you that you can give to your new guild. Though I hope you won't be leaving anytime soon."

Danny *really* hated to disappoint her, but he said, "I'm afraid I will be. Staying in one place for too long was never part of my plans. I do appreciate all the help you've given me."

She sighed. "Just doing my job."

"Speaking of, anything new come in?"

"Just one. A high profile one. Lady Shael herself posted it. She wants a scout for a trip into Fell Forest. Given your talents it might be right up your alley."

Danny nodded. "Depending on the pay, it might be at that. Thanks."

He left Emily and marched over to the job board. Danny was relieved to learn that the job had been posted. Not that there was much else available. A few local bodyguard jobs and a couple looking for help moving furniture to a new home. Was that even something adventurers did? It asked for beginners so maybe.

He grabbed Lyra's contract and started reading. It was pretty straightforward. A hundred small gold coins for a scout willing to head into Fell Forest for an indeterminate number of days. Exactly what he asked for, how nice.

Danny felt someone looming over him. He turned to find Bruno standing a couple feet away, arms crossed and looking grim. That didn't mean too much since as far as Danny had noticed, Bruno always looked grim. The big fighter didn't exude warmth, but he did seem to mean well.

"Can I help you with something?" Danny asked.

"No. I wanted to offer my congratulations on your survival. I was certain when you signed up then took a job outside the wall that you'd come back in pieces. Looks like I underestimated you."

"I won't deny that it was a bit rough, but Robi has a good team and we managed to get by. For what it's worth, on our second trip we didn't encounter a single demon either coming or going. I think the worst of the local problems have been cleared out if you're looking to get back out into the field."

Bruno nodded. "Good to know. If the merchants start posting jobs again, we'll give it serious thought."

The big man held out his bear paw of a hand. "No hard feelings."

Danny gave him a firm shake. "None at all. Best of luck whatever you decide to do."

They parted company and he headed for the door. According to the job posting, Lyra was staying at the same inn as before. It was afternoon, but hopefully they could get an early start in the morning.

◌

A short walk brought Danny once more to Lyra's inn. It was early enough that the common room was nearly empty. The bartender eyed him as he made his way to the steps up to the second floor, but made no comment. At the top of the steps he found the room number mentioned in the contract and knocked.

Lyra opened up, looked him over, and said, "How did your last job go?"

"Fine. We didn't see a single demon or monster. I suspect that dealing with the priestess also convinced any surviving demons to relocate. Either that or we got lucky."

She stepped aside and waved him in. Once the door had closed she said, "Do you know we spent almost a week in Fell Forest and we didn't encounter a single demon and the church was unguarded? Everything that's going on is beyond strange. I've given up trying to compare anything to what happened in previous cycles. One moment while I get Eve."

Danny frowned at the closed door. That was positively chatty for Lyra. He immediately mistrusted it.

When they returned, Eve couldn't look him in the eye as she passed. She just scuttled by and slipped into a chair, staring at her shoes all the while. Yeah, something was definitely going on.

"Okay," Danny said. "Who wants to tell me what's got you both acting weird?"

Eve finally looked up at him. "Adonael wants me to convince you to hunt down the demon king instead of destroying the ritual. She said it's my duty."

"Well, I told your boss and now I'm telling you, it's not happening. Lyra?"

"I don't think I was acting all that strange. I will say that Richard is withering under the pressure. He looks to have aged ten years in the past month. I don't have high hopes for his long-term health if nothing changes."

Danny shrugged. "Good. I have little sympathy for someone who wanted me killed. So what's the plan? I assume we keep it simple, head straight to the church in the morning, seal the portal, then come right back so I can get my payment?"

"Unless some other insane thing happens, that's my intention." Lyra took a rolled-up piece of parchment out of her satchel and handed it to him. "Based on the three churches we've found so far, that's a map of where I estimate the rest will be."

Danny unrolled it and frowned. If the spacing was correct, there were thirty of them all the way around the Five Kingdoms. That seemed like a lot. How long would it take them to reach each portal, shut it down, and move on to the next? It looked like a half-year job and maybe longer. That would put them in the middle of winter. At least it would assuming the seasons ran the same here as they did on Earth.

"This is a huge job. Are you sure about the numbers?"

"I'm no longer sure of anything I haven't seen with my own eyes," Lyra said. "And I'm somewhat dubious of even that. If I'm wrong and we find fewer churches than I fear, so much the better. You're going to get paid either way, so what difference does it make?"

She had a point. Danny could always leave in the spring with his pockets full of gold and a shiny new elite adventurer badge.

"Fair enough. We leave in the morning?"

Lyra nodded. "At first light."

CHAPTER 22

Fell Forest was dark and silent, just as Danny remembered. He, Lyra, and Eve had ended up walking rather than riding since they had no one to look after their mounts. Eve kept up well. All the recent action must have kept her in good shape. She had also made no attempt to change his mind about the demon king. He appreciated her discretion even as he hoped it wouldn't get her into trouble with her master. Eve was one of the few people Danny genuinely liked on this miserable world and he'd hate to see her end up on the wrong side of an archangel.

He held the unlit ethersword ready in his right hand. Despite the lack of demons, the forest was as filled with corruption as ever. Holding the mithril hilt kept the worst of the effects at bay and spared Eve from having to cast protective magic on him.

"We're getting close." Lyra whispered despite the fact that there was nothing around to hear her.

Sure enough five minutes later they strode into a clearing

and found the church, still undefended, just like Lyra had described. Danny put the ethersword away. Without a word Lyra handed him the hero's sword and he led the way into the church. Inside, he sensed no energy emerging from the black portal. It might have been a pool of ink for the threat he felt from it.

"I'll keep watch," Lyra said. "You two get busy."

Danny shot her a look, but didn't complain about the high-handed treatment. In fact, he was relieved that she'd gone back to normal.

He gathered ether, funneling it through the blade to make it pure and strong before pulling it into his body. When he reached three-quarters of his maximum, Danny placed the tip of the sword on the portal and pushed.

It resisted, but he didn't relent. Power flooded his muscles and he leaned in with all he could muster. It took half a minute but finally the tip of the sword pushed through. As soon as it did, Eve placed her hands over his and channeled divine energy into the portal.

Unlike the last time they did this, the portal closed in less than a minute. As soon as it did, Danny relaxed and let the power flow back out of him.

"That didn't seem as bad as last time," Eve said.

"Definitely not," Danny agreed. "Probably because the portal was dormant. Nice change of pace to have things go our way. Let's get out of here."

They joined Lyra out front and she quirked an eyebrow. "Done?"

Danny nodded. "Yeah, no problem."

He leveled the sword at the church and loosed a massive fireball that blew it to splinters before offering the hero's sword back to Lyra.

"You should hold on to it," she said.

"No, it's not my sword anymore. When we get to the next portal, I'll take it back, not before."

Lyra put the hero's sword into her storage, muttering all the while about stubborn humans. Maybe she was right and he was being stubborn, but Danny didn't care. Damned if he was going to do anything that might get their expectations up. He wasn't the hero anymore and that was the end of it.

They still had plenty of daylight left so the trio set out for the forest's edge. As they walked Danny asked, "Where to next?"

"About three hundred miles east. That seems to be the general spacing. After you collect your pay, we'll get some horses and ride most of the way. With no major cities nearby we'll have to return to Rosenbar's Adventurers' Guild to renew your contract. Backtracking is going to be a nuisance, but if you insist on doing it that way, we'll make the time."

Three hundred miles of extra riding didn't appeal to him. Maybe they could find some way to set up all the jobs at once then collect his money and his upgrade all at the same time.

"We'll ask Emily when we reach Rosenbar if she has some way to compact the process to save us running around."

"That would certainly be nice," Lyra said. "I know nothing about how the Adventurers' Guild works. All my time has been spent serving the throne directly."

"It's an interesting place," Danny said. "The people are helpful and generally good-natured. There's a strong sense of camaraderie with your team. It reminds me of the military back home."

The conversation trailed off after that and they hiked on in silence. Danny had no idea what to make of the absence of demons and monsters, but wasn't going to complain.

It was starting to get dark when Lyra held up a hand. "I sense something."

Danny concentrated harder. Whatever she sensed, he couldn't pick it up. Lyra always did have finer discernment than him.

They inched closer until Danny finally spotted something moving around. It looked like a man dressed in a blue uniform with a black rose on the chest. Since there was no way an ordinary soldier would be here on his own, Danny assumed it was a thrall. An especially new or stupid one since Danny was holding the ethersword and it showed no sign of reacting to the mithril.

As soon as he thought that, the thrall's head popped up like a gopher and it looked at them with burning red eyes.

Danny blasted it with a holy lance, reducing it to ash. "Pathetic. A single thrall can't possibly be the only thing in the area."

"It used to be a soldier of Forte," Lyra said. "I recognized the uniform. It probably came through the portal after their capital was destroyed. Though you're right, it hardly seems like they'd send just one."

"What should we do?" Eve was still pale and worn out from closing the portal. She'd been keeping up but just barely.

"There's nothing we can do at the moment," Lyra said. "I'll increase the power of the ward around our camp tonight and we'll see if anything shows up."

○

The trip back to Rosenbar went off without a hitch. As Danny hoped, it seemed demon activity in the area had dropped to basically nothing. He could tell from Lyra's expression she didn't trust the good news. Neither did he for that matter, but Danny also wasn't the sort to look a gift horse in the mouth. The way things had been going, the locals deserved a break.

As they made their way to the Adventurers' Guild Eve said, "Is it okay if I skip the meeting?"

"That's fine," Lyra said. "In fact, I was planning to ask you to update the temple about the current lack of demons. They can spread the word. We'll meet back at the inn."

Eve sagged with relief. "Thanks. I've never been really comfortable around adventurers."

"Have you known many?" Danny asked.

Eve frowned. "No. In fact, I'm not sure I've ever met one in person. I guess I find the idea of them uncomfortable. That's kind of pitiful, isn't it?"

"Not at all," Lyra said. "Adventurers are unreliable mercenaries who will do just about anything for money. You're right to be wary of them."

Danny looked from one to the other. "You realize I'm right here and you're bashing my new job?"

"Present company excepted," Lyra said.

Danny nodded. "That's better."

They parted ways with Eve a few minutes later and turned down the street to the guild. Danny hoped they could work something out. They had a lot of running to do and bouncing back and forth between guilds would slow them down a fair bit. On the other hand, he really wanted to get his upgrade to elite. It was an odd situation.

"Don't forget to use my new name," Danny said as they approached the front door.

"Give me a little credit," Lyra said. "That's not a mistake I'm liable to make."

"Considering your age, I was uncertain about your memory."

She shot him a glare which only made Danny grin. It was fun giving her a hard time. Especially since if she wanted his help, she had to put up with it. He doubted many people had the guts to give her shit.

Danny pushed through the door first. The waiting room was only halfway full today. That had to be a good sign. Maybe the others had finally worked up the nerve to go back out in the field, which would mean the merchants were running again as well. As long as they didn't get careless or wander too far from Rosenbar, it should be okay.

Emily's face lit up when she saw him and immediately turned serious again. No doubt Lyra's presence had a lot to do with that. She could suck the fun out of any room she entered.

Best get right to business. Danny handed Emily the signed contract.

"Did the job go smoothly?" Emily asked. Every few seconds her gaze would flick over to Lyra before returning to Danny.

"Yeah, no problem. This part of Villipan appears largely demon free now. And please try to relax. Lady Shael doesn't bite."

Emily let out a nervous little laugh. "Of course not. Let me take care of this and get your money."

"Thanks. When you're finished, there's something else we need to discuss with you."

"That sounds somewhat ominous. Just a moment." Emily moved down the counter and crouched to open the small safe. Coins jingled and a minute later she returned with a heavy pouch.

"Here you are and that's two missions down. At this rate you'll make elite in no time."

"That's the plan. Now for that other matter. Is there a way to combine multiple contracts into one?"

"I'm not sure what you mean."

"I have multiple areas I need scouted," Lyra said. "Ronin did a fine job with the first one and I wish to hire him for the rest at the same time."

Emily nodded in understanding. "And you want credit for each location like it was a separate job so you'll continue to advance without having to return to the guild each time."

"Exactly," Danny said. "This job is time sensitive, so having to ride back to the guild between stops is a problem. And spending months to get one more complete job is also a problem. So what do you think, can you help me out?"

"I think I could word the contract to give you what you want, assuming Lady Shael is willing to put such a large amount of gold up front."

"That's not a problem," Lyra said.

"Then I just need to get the guild master's approval. If you'll give me the details, I'll write up the contract and take it back to him."

Lyra ended up claiming there were twenty locations of interest. No one had any actual idea how many churches waited in Fell Forest, but that seemed like a reasonable number. If they found more, Danny was willing to seal them as a bonus since he was making out like a bandit on this deal.

When they were finished, he'd have more than enough gold to cover his traveling expenses.

"Okay," Emily said. "That should do it. You two can sit in the waiting area if you want. I shouldn't be long."

"Thanks. I appreciate you doing this." Danny offered her his best smile.

"Not at all. Taking care of adventurers is my job. I'll be right back."

Emily hurried down the hall to the guild master's office.

Danny glanced at Lyra but she showed no sign of wanting to sit down.

"She has feelings for you," Lyra said.

"Maybe, but nothing serious. We barely know each other. I'm trying not to encourage her since I'll be leaving soon. I already explained that."

"Adventurers are a transient bunch. I'm sure someone in her position is used to dealing with it."

Danny shifted closer and pitched his voice low. "How do you think that thrall got all the way here from Forte?"

"Through the portal, I assume. Sometime before it was shut down. What I can't figure out is why only one was sent or, assuming more than one was sent, where the rest are."

"I have a theory, but you won't like it."

Lyra's standard frown deepened. "I haven't liked anything that's happened since the current cycle began. Let's hear it."

"I figure the priestess in charge of that church has taken over another town and the thralls are now hiding in barns or outbuildings waiting for the order to attack. What do you want to bet they left that lone thrall in the area as an alarm? And now that it's been destroyed, they'll be on even higher alert."

"A reasonable theory given what's happened elsewhere.

And you're right, I don't like it at all. Whatever the case, it's up to Richard and the army to ferret them out. We need to focus on the job only we can do, closing the rest of the portals."

Danny had no intention of doing otherwise. He was just an employee now. Let the people in charge worry about it. "My main concern was what we might find if we walked into a village some evening looking for shelter. I'd just as soon avoid a repeat of what happened last time."

"I don't remember you being this negative before."

Danny shrugged. "That's a subject best avoided in public."

"Sorry for the wait." Emily returned to the counter with Guild Master Duret in tow.

The old man bowed to Lyra. "Lady Shael, welcome to my guildhall. I'm pleased one of my members has been of such use that you wish to retain his service for multiple jobs. It's the first time we've ever gotten such a request. While there's no reason not to grant it, there's also no precedent. It would be best if, when the contract is fulfilled, you returned here to claim your reward."

"Not a problem," Danny said. "It was always my intention to return this fall. Trevor's son is departing on a grand caravan and I'm thinking of joining him."

Duret's dour expression brightened. "A fine way to see the world. I've heard tales of grand caravans, but never had the chance to join one. I'm somewhat jealous of you."

If he knew the whole truth Danny figured he'd be a fair bit less jealous.

Lyra cleared her throat. "If we could move this along."

"I beg your pardon," Duret said. "Everything's in order. We just need the two thousand small gold pieces for the deposit."

Lyra opened her storage, pulled out two heavy leather sacks, and plunked them down on the counter. "There you are. I trust two hundred large gold coins will serve as well."

Duret turned to Danny. "Would you like us to count it and confirm the amount?"

"I'm confident Lady Shael wouldn't try and cheat me."

"In that case, we're all set." Duret handed the contract to Danny. "When you return, I'll be happy to upgrade you to elite. You'll have more than earned it."

"I appreciate you indulging my odd request."

"Not at all. It's a great honor for a member of the guild to have a chance to work for the Champion of Villipan."

When Danny glanced at Lyra he would've sworn she was blushing.

CHAPTER 23

I f not for the whole demon-infestation thing, riding across the Villipan countryside in late summer would've been pleasant. At least, that was what Danny thought as he cut the head off the last lamprey demon. The ugly things were the most common sort of full demon they ran into, which was strange for a demon lord who was supposed to be all about beauty.

They were a week out of Rosenbar and riding generally northeast. In that time they'd already encountered three groups of demons. They were all weak and died easily, but that seemed like a lot considering how peaceful it was further west.

Danny deactivated the ethersword and turned to Lyra. She was standing over the dissolving corpse of her own defeated enemy. For her part, Eve was hiding with the horses inside a holy barrier. This was at Danny's request. He didn't want to have to worry about her while he was fighting.

Eve let the barrier vanish and asked, "Are you both okay?"

"I'm fine," he said. "Thoroughly sick of these things, but

otherwise fine. We're in the middle of nowhere. Why are they so thick?"

Lyra shrugged and sheathed her sword. For some reason she was reluctant to wield the hero's sword herself. Danny didn't care enough to ask why, but it did strike him as strange. "I wish I knew why demons did half the things they did. They're chaos and destruction incarnate. You have to accept that people like us will never understand them. And if you meet a human who does, beware."

Having met the sexy demon nuns, Danny was well aware of how crazy they were. He was about to suggest they get going when he heard something. He cocked his head and enhanced his hearing. "Do you hear that? Sounds like a battle."

"Yes, it does," Lyra said. "We should ride around it. These fights are slowing us down."

"We can't do that," Eve said. "Someone might need our help. We need to take a look."

Danny stayed silent. He was, happily, nothing but a hired scout now. If they wanted to look, he'd look; if not, that was okay too.

The two women were glaring at each other, neither willing to give an inch. Danny didn't bother pointing out that it would be faster to just look than to stand here doing nothing. His father had told him many times that the best thing a man could do, when confronted by an argument between women, was to keep out of it.

The standoff dragged on until Danny could no longer hear sounds of battle. "It's over."

"Good," Lyra said. "Problem solved."

She swung into her saddle.

"We should still go look." Eve mounted up as well. "Someone might be hurt."

"Fine, but we don't linger."

Danny smiled to himself as he climbed onto the back of his horse. Eve was remarkably stubborn about some things and she almost always got her way. Maybe it was a high priestess thing. Nobody wanted to piss off the healer.

They guided their mounts up and over a low hill. On the other side the battlefield was visible. Dead crimson ogres were mingled with puddles of dissolving demons. Twenty fully armored knights sat on their horses. Another dozen littered the ground but showed no spark of life.

"Curse the luck," Lyra muttered. "That's Alban Morel's unit. What's he doing here? I know for a fact he was deployed to the south. Well, I guess I shouldn't be surprised he ignored his orders. Since we're either in or near the Morels' duchy it's no wonder he came here given how many demons we've run into. And here comes the idiot now."

Sure enough, a small group of six knights was riding their way. They didn't have their weapons drawn which was a good sign.

Lyra glanced at Danny, who shrugged and offered a rueful smile. "No way will he recognize me now. Let's get this over with. The less time I have to spend in the man's company, the better I'll like it."

"At last," Lyra said. "Something none of us is going to argue about."

"Lady Shael." Alban's snooty voice had a weird sort of echo coming out of his helmet. "This is unexpected. What are you doing in Morel Duchy?"

"I'm on my way to a section of Fell Forest where we

suspect excess demon activity. What about you? It was my understanding that His Majesty ordered your knights south."

"Indeed, indeed, that was the plan. But my brother contacted me about increased demon activity at home so I returned at once. And it's well that I did. We can't have Villipan's most important duchy fall to the enemy."

While they talked, Danny looked the knights over. He didn't expect to find anything, but checking for psychic interference had become a habit. And it was well that it had. Alban and his knights had all been placed under some sort of spell. Danny couldn't tell what it did, but it was different than any of the spells he'd seen before.

"I see you've got High Priestess Carre with you, but who's this other fellow?" Alban asked.

"An adventurer with some skill as a scout," Lyra said. "His name is Ronin."

Danny offered a polite bow from the back of his horse but didn't speak. This was both because commoners weren't supposed to speak to a noble unless addressed directly and because Danny didn't want to risk Alban recognizing his voice. An unlikely prospect given their brief interaction, but not impossible.

"I'm sure you need to get back to your patrols," Lyra said. "And we have our own mission to complete. Good day."

"Don't be so hasty." Alban moved his mount to block Lyra's. "Maxime would never forgive me if I didn't bring you to the castle for a visit when you're so close. Surely your task isn't so urgent that you'd offend my brother."

Lyra grimaced. If Danny remembered right, Duke Morel was one of the few people in the kingdom she didn't want to piss off. Had she noticed that the knights had been ensorcelled? Danny had no idea and no way to find out that wouldn't tip his hand. At a minimum, he felt certain, if they went with Alban, they would be walking into a trap.

"Fine," Lyra said at last. "A brief visit to pay our respects won't cost us too much time. And I certainly have no desire to offend Duke Morel."

"Excellent. It's only two days to the castle. My men need to resupply anyways, so this is perfect for us as well. Get the others! We're leaving."

"The bodies need to be dealt with first," Eve said. "If you leave them lying around, they could be turned into thralls or undead. They need to be burned."

Alban scowled, an expression that gave his stern face a cruel twist. He looked like he wanted to argue, but Eve was right and he had to know that. "Of course, Lady Carre. In my excitement it slipped my mind. If I could trouble Lady Shael for the loan of her magic, we can deal with them quickly."

"Not a problem," Lyra said. "Have your men gather the bodies into a pile and I'll incinerate them."

The group rode back toward the battlefield. Danny wanted to talk to Lyra but Alban never moved far enough away to let them speak privately. She had to know something weird was going on. Lyra was too clever and experienced not to automatically check everyone they met. They'd run into far too many brainwashed people for it to be otherwise. If she was playing along, she had to have a reason.

The knights got to work, dragging the human bodies over to the ogres. As they worked, Danny looked closely at the human bodies. Some of them had been crushed or burned by hellfire, but several others had been killed by swords. At least he assumed they had been based on their nearly severed heads. As far as he could tell there were no wizards in

Alban's group, which meant he would've had no chance of defeating the demons.

Every way Danny turned it, he could only come up with one answer for what he saw: the knights were in the service of the demons.

Lyra and Eve gave no sign that they'd come to a similar conclusion. Not that any of them could give away the game if the plan was to play along until they reached the castle.

"Hey!" Alban's sharp word jolted Danny out of his thoughts. "You might lend a hand."

"I was hired to be a scout not a day laborer," Danny said, keeping his tone gruff.

"Why, you arrogant peon." Alban reached for his sword.

Danny kept his expression impassive. "I know my rights and duties as an adventurer. If it's not in the contract, I don't have to do it. And handling corpses like some necromancer's assistant is definitely not in my contract."

"He's right," Lyra said. "You know the rules of the guild and how they relate to the nobility. Do you want to convince the adventurers to leave Villipan? Do you have any idea how many odd jobs they handle that are either too small for the army or completely beyond our awareness? It would be chaos."

Alban moved his hand away from his sword. "Fine. The rest of you get back to work!"

The knights that had paused to listen to the argument resumed dragging bodies around. The humans were stripped of weapons and armor before being added to the pile. At last Lyra stepped in and a stream of flames shot from her hand.

It took about an hour to reduce the corpses to ash. Once they were done, the group mounted their horses and set out east and a little south. Getting dragged on this side trip

THE BIRTH OF RONIN

didn't appeal to him, but Danny wanted his pay and would play along however he had to in order to get it.

○

Danny and the rest of his group only managed a few more miles before dusk. Alban called a halt and the knights got busy setting up camp in a field. Alban, naturally, had someone else put up his tent while he looked around with his nose stuck in the air. Danny kept his distance and pitched a one-person tent.

When he noticed Eve struggling with hers, he walked over and asked, "Need a hand?"

"Thank you."

Danny took a knee beside her and whispered, "You saw the spell woven into their minds, right?"

Eve nodded and adjusted one of the stakes before Danny drove it into the ground with a hatchet.

"Do you know what Lyra's planning?"

"No, we haven't had a chance to talk. They're keeping an awfully close eye on us."

Speaking of which, a pair of knights moved closer, ending the conversation. It took only a minute for Danny to finish setting up Eve's tent. When he stood, he looked over at Lyra, but Alban was only a few feet away. No chance for a private chat now.

Well, whatever. Despite her betrayal he still trusted her not to sell him out to the demons.

No one bothered starting a fire so they ended up gnawing on cold jerky. Not Danny's first choice for a meal, but damned if he was going to offer to cook for this many people.

When they'd finished their meager repast Alban said, "My knights will split the watch. Lady Shael and Lady Carre should get their sleep. Wouldn't want to be exhausted when we reach the castle."

If this clown thought Danny was going to trust his knights, then he was dumber than he looked. Before he lay down, Danny wove wards around his and Eve's tents. He would've done Lyra's as well, but she beat him to it. When he saw her casting, she looked up and gave him the faintest of nods. Exactly what it meant he didn't know, but he assumed it was some sort of reassurance that she knew what was happening and had a plan.

Was it an overly optimistic assumption? Maybe, but given her centuries of experience, Danny was confident Alban Morel wouldn't get the best of her on his best day. His preparations made, Danny crawled into his tent and closed his eyes.

Three hours later, his ward triggered. He slid out of the tent to find a trio of knights standing paralyzed three feet from his tent. They had their weapons drawn, making it perfectly clear what they intended. A glance toward Eve's tent revealed a similar scene. As far as he could tell, she was still sound asleep.

Lyra, on the other hand, had already emerged from her tent, sword drawn, and was stalking across the clearing toward Alban, who stood surrounded by the rest of the knights. Even if she could take them all on her own, Danny figured it was best to lend a hand.

He activated his stealth field and got silently to his feet. Swinging wide around the knights, Danny approached Alban from behind. His dagger didn't make a sound when it slid out of its sheath. If Lyra needed help, Danny would be ready.

"What are you playing at, Alban?" Lyra asked. "Thinking you could send assassins in the middle of the night is remarkably stupid even for you. Surely you didn't think I'd just trust you."

"Of course not," Alban said with remarkable calm. "Though if it had worked, I would've been well pleased. Disposing of traitors to the Crown is my job after all."

Lyra looked confused and Danny knew how she felt. What was this dipshit going on about?

"The only traitor here is you. A blind person could tell you murdered three of those knights."

"You won't confuse me with your lies. We know the royal family and all those outside of Morel Duchy have been replaced by demonic servants. The true high priestess of Adonael brought a warning to my brother. I can only assume that the real Lady Shael has been slain and her body destroyed. A pity, her help reclaiming the kingdom would've made the task much easier. It's time for you and the other traitors to die."

Danny had heard enough. He took a single stride and canceled his stealth field as he brought his dagger to Alban's throat. "You might want to rethink your plan. Unless you're eager to die as well."

"Alban," Lyra said. "Describe the priestess."

When Alban didn't speak Danny pressed hard enough to draw blood. "You heard the lady. Talk."

"She was beautiful. Dark hair, a lush figure—everyone that saw her was instantly smitten, including my brother. Had she declared herself a goddess, we wouldn't have doubted it. But she said that she was only a humble priestess come to warn us of the great danger we faced. She said only our strength and wisdom could save Villipan. I've been doing my best to hunt down and slay all the traitors in the duchy. Once it's secure, we can move on to the neighboring lands."

Danny could only marvel at the level of stupidity and arrogance on display. Clearly one of the sexy nuns had enchanted everyone at Morel Castle. Though given what she had to work with, she no doubt could've convinced them with words alone.

"You can't hold me prisoner forever and as soon as you let me go, my men will cut you down," Alban said. "Best if you accept your fate. It will be less painful if you do."

"I have an alternate plan." Ether gathered around Lyra then surged out. Every knight save Alban collapsed, unconscious but alive.

Danny could feel Alban trembling. He must not have realized that the knights weren't dead. "Even if you kill me, there are other groups out hunting traitors. You can't escape us all."

Lyra moved closer.

Alban tried to shrink away but Danny refused to allow it.

"I need some information and the easiest way to get it is to pluck it straight out of what passes for your brain. Unless you want that useless organ reduced to mush, don't resist."

The trembling grew worse and Danny feared Alban might cut his own throat. He assumed that would make it harder for Lyra to do whatever she was going to do, so he eased the pressure on his dagger blade.

She reached out and touched his forehead. Alban went absolutely rigid.

Danny stepped back and checked on the knights. They showed no sign of waking up and he couldn't sense any corruption in the area. It seemed their camp was safe for the moment.

Lyra's spell lasted about five minutes and when she finished Alban fell face first to the ground.

"What did you learn?" Danny asked.

"More than I wanted to know about Alban's fantasies. As far as relevant information, there's definitely a priestess of Ardent Lilly at their castle. She also has several attendants that are likely demons in disguise."

"Okay. How does this affect our mission to seal the portals?"

"Other than having to avoid the other patrols, it doesn't. However, I'm hoping I can convince you to help me kill the priestess and free Maxime and his retainers."

"Why would I volunteer to rescue people who I'm pretty sure already hated me when I was the hero? Let the demons have them, they deserve each other."

"I can't argue with anything you said, however, the Morels, pitiful excuses for humans that they are, can still cause a lot of trouble for the kingdom, especially under the control of demons. Their knights are already out killing innocents. They need to be stopped."

"Stopped dead or freed from demon control?"

"Freed would be ideal, but stopped one way or the other. Will you help me?"

"Fine, but I expect a bonus when the contract is fulfilled. I signed up to close portals, not rescue idiot nobles. Speaking of, what about these clowns? They're bound to wake up sooner or later. Can't say I'm terribly enthusiastic about having them riding to the demons' rescue."

"That's not a problem," Lyra said. "We'll take their horses with us. The fight will be over before they even reach the castle."

"It pains me to say this, but Alban and his men are apt to

end up like the villagers I helped rescue—unconscious in a heap somewhere. If anyone cares to look, it might be kind of hard to find them."

"Fair point, but I don't have enough rope to tie them all up and leaving them here is like advertising them as demon food. I think we'll have to risk it."

"Your call, I was just pointing out it might be an issue. Will they be out until morning? I need to get some sleep."

"Go ahead. I'll stay awake and make sure nothing happens. Elf-bloods need less sleep than humans anyway."

Danny wasn't about to argue. He crawled back into his tent and renewed the ward. He couldn't help thinking as he dozed off that Eve had to be the soundest sleeper he'd ever met.

CHAPTER 24

D uke Morel's castle sat on a hill overlooking a fair-sized town. A steep, winding road led to an outer wall Danny guessed stood about forty feet high. The only way inside was a heavy gate made of thick wood, guarded by ten knights on the ground and archers on the battlements above. Beyond the wall waited the main keep, a massive stone fortress covered with arrow slits. All in all it was an impressive fortification. Against a normal enemy it would doubtless prove a huge challenge.

Unfortunately for the duke and his new demon masters, Danny was far from an ordinary enemy. The plan Lyra came up with was for him to sneak inside while she approached from the front. Eve was at their inn. Danny liked the kind-hearted high priestess, but her combat abilities were basically nonexistent. Better for everyone if she kept her distance until the battle was over. On the plus side, everyone they'd checked in town was free from demonic influence.

For the moment anyway. He assumed there had to be some sort of limiting principle when it came to how many people any given person could control. If he was right, then the priestess would have to bring in reinforcements to control everyone. Assuming, of course, she didn't have them all killed. Since they were dealing with demon worshippers, it would be foolish in the extreme to take the people's safety for granted.

And that was really why Danny was going along with this. Now that his anger toward Lyra and her masters in the capital had cooled, he recognized it wasn't right to let the innocent people of Villipan suffer for the stupidity of their rulers.

He reached the base of the wall and banished all extraneous thoughts from his mind. It was time to get down to business. He sent ether into his legs and leapt. It was a near thing, but he got one hand on the battlement and pulled himself up.

An archer stood ten feet away and didn't even flinch at Danny's arrival. Sometimes he thought his stealth field was unfair, but today he was glad to have it. A quick glance confirmed that the archer had been enchanted. No doubt anyone capable of fighting had been.

Danny knew nothing about Duke Morel's family beyond Alban being a member. He figured the guy had to have a wife and a couple of kids. None of whom would have any value to a demon priestess. Hopefully the worst hadn't happened and they were being held prisoner somewhere. That was what Danny was supposed to find out. Freeing any potential hostages was necessary before the final confrontation.

Leaving the archer none the wiser, Danny hopped down from the wall, landing on a cushion of conjured air. The courtyard was empty. Where were the soldiers training? A blacksmith should be working on something. He didn't even hear any horse noises coming from the stable. The silence was jarring.

He shrugged and made a quick tour of the outbuildings. As he expected, the stable was empty as was the smithy. Maybe Alban had all the horses. No, that didn't make any sense. The people at the castle needed some way to get around.

He found a storage building filled with tools, but no groundskeepers. Danny shook his head. Trying to figure this out was going to give him a headache. All that mattered was finding any people that hadn't been dominated and getting them somewhere safe.

He crept up to the keep. Six knights guarded the entrance. Invisible or not, they'd have to be blind not to notice Danny opening the door. Knocking them out would be easy, but that was likely to draw attention as well.

Then again, maybe it wouldn't. They were just standing there. It wouldn't take much magic to prop them in place while they were unconscious.

The ether instantly responded to his mental image. All six men went rigid, their eyes open but seeing nothing. Perfect, as long as you disregarded the creepy wide-eyed stares.

Now for the door. He gave it a push but of course it was barred from the inside. Cutting it open would work, but if it was barred, that meant there had to be guards inside to unbar it. Man, he wished he could just kick the door down, toss in a grenade, and go in guns blazing.

But that wasn't the job. He'd done hostage rescue a couple of times and it was always one of the harder missions. Dealing with nothing but hostiles was so much simpler.

Best to go with the direct approach. Danny slammed his

fist into the door a couple of times and a voice called out, "What is it?"

Danny didn't bother answering. Using psychic magic of his own, he grabbed ahold of the guard's mind and had him open the door.

"What are you doing?" a second voice asked.

Danny zapped him the same way he did the guards outside. A moment later the door opened and he walked through. One rigid guard stood directly ahead of him staring at nothing while his partner held the door open.

"Close it," Danny said.

The guard obeyed then stared at him, or at the space he was occupying, since Danny was still invisible, waiting for another order like a good magical slave. So creepy.

When he was well away from the entrance, Danny released all the spells he'd used. The soldiers would have slight headaches and the one he controlled would add a short gap in his memory to that. The rest would be confused, but hopefully just dismiss it as some weird, random thing. When your castle was under the control of demon worshippers, weird, random things had to happen all the time.

His infiltration complete, Danny slipped through the empty, silent halls like a ghost. Much like outside, it was eerily silent. The spike in background corruption did nothing to help Danny's nerves. He wanted to take out the ethersword in the worst way, but feared having the mithril in the open would alert the demons to his presence. For now he'd have to suck it up and keep moving.

He passed a number of closed doors. There was no life force behind any of them and so he kept moving. The side halls appeared abandoned but when he reached the central corridor he sensed a life force. Not an especially large one, but it was the only thing of note he'd come across so far.

The source of the life force turned out to be in the castle's... meeting hall, maybe? It looked like a throne room, but dukes didn't have thrones, only the king did, or so his inherited memories said. Still, if this wasn't a throne room it did a credible impression of one. An angry-looking middle-aged man sat in a big chair while a beautiful dark-haired woman stood beside him, whispering in his ear. A double row of knights lined the path to the chair. Given the corruption oozing out of them, Danny was pretty sure they were thralls.

Were Maxime Morel and the demon nun the only living people inside the castle? He hated to think so, but it looked that way.

Danny slipped away from the entrance and found a set of stairs up to the second floor. A quick search confirmed the absence of anything living outside of a few mice. That left the basement.

Or, more likely, dungeon. Part of him hoped he'd find a bunch of still-living people in cells waiting to be rescued. The larger part knew he was being stupid and that he should instead prepare himself for something awful.

He found the stairs down not far from the kitchen. The first room was a root cellar filled with moldy potatoes and other things he didn't look too closely at. A heavy wooden door separated the storage area from the dungeon he expected. A number of empty cells fitted with thick doors that only had a small, barred window to let in light lined the hallway. Like the second floor, he sensed nothing alive.

Instead, he found a huge amount of corruption. The most he'd encountered since Demon King Castle. Whatever the demons were doing, it was super deluxe extra evil. Part of him didn't want to see what was happening while the rest knew he had to.

Steeling himself, he pushed the connecting door open. The dungeon beyond had been transformed into a single large chamber. A rust-red magic circle had been drawn on the floor with what Danny was pretty sure was blood. It glowed, dull and ugly, in the dark. The stink of rotting flesh hung thick in the air, making him glad he'd skipped breakfast. The symbol pulsed with power, like it had a heartbeat of its own.

Despite the light, most of the chamber was hidden by shadows. Danny agitated the ether and conjured a light.

Not one of his better ideas. Bodies hung by chains from the ceiling, their throats cut, and all the blood drained from them. That confirmed how the magic circle was drawn. Danny's host hadn't studied magic circles to amount to anything so he had no idea what the circle did. His guess was something horrible and evil.

A vibration ran through the floor and the glow grew brighter. Well, looked like he was about to find out what it did.

CHAPTER 25

Lyra trudged up the twisting road to Duke Morel's castle. She'd given Daniel a fifteen-minute head start, which should be plenty. She still hadn't gotten completely used to working with someone she'd killed. It was strange in every way and yet natural at the same time. While he was nowhere near as friendly as he used to be, Daniel remained professional. He was a soldier to his core and she respected that. Even better, he seemed to bear the people of Villipan no ill will even if he did hate the royals.

Had their positions been reversed, Lyra would've felt the same. She swallowed a sigh and glanced at the castle. From this distance everything looked fine. If she hadn't run into Alban, she never would've guessed anything was wrong. They'd likely have reached the next portal by now and whatever was happening here would've gone on without interference.

It was a scary thought and she couldn't help wondering what else was going on in the kingdom that she didn't know about. She feared the answer was a lot.

The soldiers at the gate snapped to attention as she approached. On the battlements above, the archers had their longbows strung and arrows nocked. At least the weapons weren't pointed at her. Not that they would've had a chance of penetrating her magical shield, but that didn't make getting shot at any more enjoyable.

"Can we help you, ma'am?" asked an older soldier with a guard sergeant's band around his right arm. His mind had been modified with demon magic.

"My name is Lyra Shael. I encountered Lord Alban in the field and he suggested that I pay my respects to his brother."

"Lady Shael! It's an honor to have you here. If I could trouble you to wait a moment, I'll send word to the keep. I'm sure his lordship will be pleased to welcome you."

Lyra smiled as if she believed that for a second. "Thank you. I look forward to the duke's welcome."

A younger guard was dispatched through the gate at a run. They were making a good show of everything being normal. Anyone incapable of seeing the ether wouldn't guess anything was wrong. Had any nobles come visiting only to end up in a trap? Probably not given the state of the country-side. Hardly anyone was traveling at the moment.

"Have things been quiet around here?" Lyra asked. "Alban mentioned increased demon activity when we spoke."

"There's been no trouble at the castle, ma'am, but we've heard rumors of attacks on outlying villages. Lord Alban will set 'em straight, never fear." He said that last bit like the idea of Alban Morel doing anything would make someone feel better. The statement by itself would've been enough to confirm for her that something was wrong.

"I'm sure he will. King Richard has great confidence in Lord Alban." Lyra nearly choked on the words but she must have succeeded in sounding believable since the guards all grinned and nodded like she was talking about their prized progeny.

Thankfully, their lying contest came to an end with the return of the messenger. "Duke Morel sends his welcome and bids you join him in the great hall. I'll guide you."

"Thank you." She nodded to the sergeant and followed the young man inside. As they approached the keep she said, "I hope I'm not troubling His Grace."

"Not at all. Things have been very quiet here. I'm sure Duke Morel will be glad for the distraction."

Another group of guards had the keep door open as they approached. Lyra nodded to them in passing. As she did, she looked at them through the ether. As she expected, the magic was present, but it had also been modified. That would be Daniel's work. There was no other way into the keep short of smashing through a wall. And while she had no doubt he could do so should it be necessary, it wouldn't exactly be stealthy.

The keep door closed behind them with a rather ominous thud. She allowed no concern to show on her face. Lyra projected calm and confidence. No one that saw her would ever guess she knew she was walking into a trap.

Her footfalls echoed through the silent halls. There wasn't a servant to be seen, or any other guards. It was all wrong. Her guide kept glancing back at her.

Out of curiosity she asked, "Is everything alright? Seems a bit quiet in here."

"Yes, Lady Shael. Lord Morel likes things quiet and the servants out of sight when he doesn't need them."

It was such a ridiculous statement that she had to bite off a laugh. Had she wandered into another reality? Maybe

Ardent Lilly had a sense of humor and this was all some huge joke. Lyra had never been accused of liking a good joke, but in this case she'd be willing to make an exception.

She didn't bother with further conversation and soon they stood in front of the doors to the great hall. A double row of ten thralls lined the path up to Maxime's chair. He sat there, dressed in black and tan, a bored, vacant look on his face. His eyes, normally as sharp as razors, appeared dull and listless.

Beside him stood one of the demon priestesses. Dressed in a revealing black outfit, the woman smiled at Lyra, her eyes flashing red, as if daring her to walk through the gauntlet of thralls.

Lyra glanced at her guide who shivered and said, "I'll be leaving you here, Lady Shael."

And with that he hurried away as quickly as he could. Magically controlled or not, the young man's sense of self-preservation remained intact. It was a heartening thought.

She took a moment to strengthen her shield then strode forward. None of the thralls so much as flinched in her direction as she passed and then she stood in front of the duke.

Lyra offered a modest bow. "Duke Morel. Your younger brother suggested I pay my respects, so here I am."

"Is Alban dead?" Maxime's words came out slowly, as if it took all he had to force them past his lips.

"He wasn't when we parted company." She was getting sick of playing this game but decided on one more question. "What's happening in your castle? It feels a bit lifeless."

The priestess laughed, a cruel, humorless sound that would've been more at home on the lips of a true demon. "I had such plans for this place. Your unfortunate arrival has

THE BIRTH OF RONIN

cut my work short. Still, I believe I've gotten far enough along to give you a bit of entertainment."

Before Lyra could speak, the priestess drove her straightened fingers through Maxime's back and out his chest. Blood gushed from his mouth and wound.

Seconds later the ether stirred and roared as corruption from below came surging up through the castle. Lyra barely had a chance to raise a divine barrier before a wave of darkness washed over her.

CHAPTER 26

D anny retrieved the ethersword from storage and conjured a barrier an instant before a wave of corruption exploded out of the circle and washed over him. Despite his protections it still made his stomach twist. It was a horrible feeling and he'd be happy to never experience it again, though given his current job, that seemed unlikely.

Through the darkness he could barely make out figures moving around. They didn't move like people. The hunched-over things shambled around with a stumbling gait. Danny couldn't make out any details, but considering where they came from, he assumed they were demons of some sort.

And in his experience, the only good demon was a dead one.

One of the figures stumbled closer. Danny lit the ether-sword and swung, cutting it in half.

By the light of the blade he saw the very human face of a woman in her twenties with the typical blond hair and blue eyes of a citizen of Villipan. Her dress was ragged and an apron covered the front. Had to be one of the servants that had been hanging from the ceiling.

Did the spell raise the dead rather than summon a demon? Danny's host didn't know and Lyra hadn't bothered to teach him much about this sort of spell. He had no idea how to close the portal on his own and it was still gushing darkness like a new oil well.

Time to get out of here.

He backed away, never taking his eyes off the shuffling undead. They ignored him. It was like they had no will of their own, luckily for him.

When the door pull hit him in the butt, Danny reached behind him, yanked it open, and slipped back into the storage area. He slammed the door shut and used earth magic to fuse rock and wood together. The door was now part of the wall. That should buy him a little time. Time to do what, he was less certain.

Maybe Lyra would have a plan. She always seemed to.

Danny ran for the stairs. She had to be here by now and if she was, the fake throne room was the most likely place to find her. He retraced his steps, keeping the lit sword in his hand. Stealth served no purpose now. He rounded a corner and found himself face to face with a pair of guards that had been turned into thralls. The glowing red eyes were a dead giveaway.

They managed a single step toward him before Danny closed the gap and sliced them both in half. A second swing removed their heads, ending their thrashing.

Much as he didn't want to, Danny took a closer look at their faces. He was pretty sure these were the same ones he'd tricked into opening the keep door. The corruption wave must have killed them, allowing demon spirits to take over their bodies. It felt safe to assume all the guards outside had suffered a similar fate.

He shook his head. What a miserable waste. However much he hated demons, it wasn't enough.

Right, focus.

He left the bodies where they lay and started running. It wasn't far to the throne room and when he rounded the bend he found Lyra surrounded by twenty thralls. One of them looked like Maxime Morel. There was no sign of the nun. Wherever she'd gone, Danny assumed she was up to no good.

He gathered ether, ran it through the mithril hilt, then sent it back out as a beam of holy energy. The white light washed over the thralls and burned them to ash. In about ten seconds, only Lyra remained in the throne room.

"Nice timing," Lyra said. "Twenty thralls are a lot even for me. Where's the priestess?"

"No clue. She was gone when I arrived. Looks like all the still-living guards have been transformed into thralls. There's also a big, ugly spell circle in the basement that's the cause of all this. The thing is gushing corruption like mad."

"The servants?"

Danny shook his head. "They fed 'em to the circle. Looks like they've been turned into zombies."

Lyra frowned. "Not thralls?"

"Their eyes didn't glow, so I assume not. You'd know better than I would. Want to go take a look?"

"Later. We need to find the priestess. She has to be the key to stopping this madness. She killed the duke which triggered the magic."

"Is that strange? I mean stranger than usual."

"No, using a burst of life energy as a spark to activate a

THE BIRTH OF RONIN

spell isn't unusual for demonic magic. The bigger question is, what is she planning to do with all the corruption now?"

"Something evil I'm sure. I can't track her life force with so much corruption fouling the ether. Any thoughts on how we find her?"

"If you didn't run into her on your way here, we can assume she's not in the basement. I doubt she's on the first floor, which leaves the second. We'll just have to search until we find her."

Not the best plan he'd ever heard, but Danny couldn't come up with anything better.

They barely took a step toward the hall when an explosion shook the castle with such force Danny barely stayed on his feet.

"What the hell now?" he asked.

They abandoned the plan to search upstairs and ran for the exit. As soon as they were outside, Danny spun and looked up at the castle.

One of the towers had been smashed off. Flying above the castle was a black blob with wings and tentacles dangling from its belly. A single figure stood on the thing's back. It had to be the nun.

"That doesn't look like a demon from Ardent Lilly's hell," Lyra said. "It doesn't fit her aesthetic at all—too ugly."

"Since one of her priestesses is riding on its back, I'm going to assume it came from there and that she has flexible beauty standards. Any thoughts on how we stop it? I don't know any flying spells."

"Neither do I. Shit, here come the guards."

They stood back to back as the transformed guards ran toward them. A couple of arrows arced in as well, but their magical shields were more than enough to turn those aside.

The ethersword made quick work of the first thralls to reach him. Danny grimaced as he cut down the newly made thralls. Aside from their eyes, they might have been still-living men. But whatever they might have been, they were currently trying their best to kill Danny and Lyra and needed to be dealt with.

The weak things had no hope of success and soon they'd been reduced to unmoving corpses. The flying demon, on the other hand, was now hovering over the nearby town. As Danny watched, its belly tentacles shot down.

"I know what that thing is," Lyra said. "It's a life breaker. It'll snatch people up, take them into its body, drain their life force, and spit them out as thralls. If we don't stop it, the demon could transform the entire town before moving on to the next one."

"I'm all in favor of stopping it," Danny said. "Just tell me how."

"We'll have to try and burn it away bit by bit with holy lances."

Danny frowned. "That'll take forever. If you can stop the tentacles, I'll hit it with one huge blast. But I need time to build up a charge. Say two minutes?"

She nodded. "I'll save as many people as I can. Good luck."

Danny would take all he could get.

CHAPTER 27

Eve sat in a pew in the otherwise empty temple of Adonael and sighed. She hated being left behind even as she knew she'd be a liability on a combat mission. If they'd had a larger group and could dedicate someone to protect her, that would be another matter, but with just Daniel and Lady Shael, it was impossible. And so here she sat, waiting for her friends—maybe companions would be a better word; Lady Shael didn't seem interested in being friends and Daniel was still too angry—to return.

To be fair, he was still polite and considerate, just more distant than before.

Eve looked to the white-cloth-draped altar. Why had Adonael allowed the hero, the man who Eve believed carried the archangel's blessing, to be killed, over and over? It made no sense. A small part of Eve had wanted to ask that very question when she stood before Adonael, but the rest of her was too overwhelmed to force the words out. Did that make Eve a coward? Probably. But a priestess couldn't just blurt out a question like that. At a minimum it was rude and at worst could be interpreted as a lack of faith.

She felt completely inadequate and a little disgusted with her weakness. Eve firmed her resolve. She'd find some way to make a difference, she swore it.

As if seeking to test her determination, a massive spike of corruption hit her magical senses. Eve leapt to her feet and ran for the door. It didn't take a genius to figure out where that came from.

Out in the street she turned to face the castle. All around her, people were doing the same. Even if they couldn't see the ether, such a powerful burst of corruption would be noticeable to almost anyone close to the source.

Eve's jaw dropped. A black portal opened above the castle and a many-tentacled thing emerged from it. It didn't have a head or tail or anything to give it a sense of shape. It was just a dark blob with dangling tentacles. Somehow its lack of shape made it even more horrific.

She squinted. Was someone standing on its back?

As she tried to comprehend what was happening, the creature turned toward the town and began to approach. As soon as it did, people started screaming.

Eve knew what she had to do. Using magic to amplify her voice she said, "Head for the temple! Adonael will protect us. Hurry!"

A few people stopped running and looked at her. Eve waved them into the temple.

She kept shouting and waving, trying to get as many people inside as she could before the demon arrived. There was no way to protect everyone; the temple was too small and the time before the demon arrived too short. But Eve was determined to save as many as she could.

The temple was packed with people by the time she finally gave up and joined them. She forced her way through the gathering and stood in front of the altar. Only three priests lived at this temple and all of them had emerged from the living quarters in the back to stand with her.

"Everyone, please!" Eve shouted to get their attention. "Bow your heads and join me in asking for Adonael's protection."

She followed her own advice and out of the corner of her eye saw the other priests had followed suit. She began the traditional prayer for guidance, modifying it as she went to ask for protection instead. After the second time through, every voice in the temple was chanting along with her.

The darkness from outside was slowly replaced by divine energy. Eve guided it to form a bubble around the temple. They'd done it, though for how long, she couldn't say.

◌

Lyra sprinted toward the bizarre demon as it hovered over the town. A bolt of lightning arced out from her finger only to fizzle on some sort of corrupt barrier. The demon didn't even flinch. Lyra wasn't used to her magic failing or being ignored by her enemies. It was insulting, and she meant to make both the demon and its master pay for their arrogance.

Behind her Daniel's magic built steadily. He needed two minutes. That had seemed like a short time when he said it but right now it felt like ages.

Some of the guards on wall duty shot arrows at the demon.

They might as well have thrown insults for all the good they did.

Tentacles shot down, wrapped them up, and yanked them into the demon's body. A few seconds later the guards were dropped unceremoniously to the ground.

Lyra finally caught up, leapt the wall without pausing, and landed inside. The fallen guards had regained their feet and all six stared at her with glowing red eyes. The newly born thralls ran at her, their arming swords burning with corrupt flames.

She ducked and dodged, cutting the demons down with ease. As she fought, more tentacles shot down, smashing through roofs and pulling more people out of their homes and up into its body. All too soon, more thralls rained down to the ground.

As soon as she finished off the guards, the transformed townsfolk came running at her. They weren't even armed, but they fought without fear using only their fists. Cutting them down took no particular effort, but more were being made all the time.

What was taking Daniel so long? Surely it had been two minutes by now.

As soon as she thought that, the largest holy lance she'd ever seen came blazing across the sky. An instant before it struck, a dark barrier appeared, shielding the demon.

Dark and light battled until finally the barrier shattered and the lance blasted through. When it faded, half the demon had been burned away. The priestess, unfortunately, appeared unharmed. She pointed and the demon got back to work.

Lyra didn't even have time to curse as she kept fighting.

She'd been so certain Daniel could take it out with a single shot. So much for her faith.

$$\circ$$

Danny stared in disbelief. He would've sworn that holy lance had power enough to vaporize ten demons, yet the one he'd just blasted had survived. Or, some of it survived. He burned away about half of its mass, but the rest was already back to grabbing people. He debated blasting it again, but if the first shot wasn't enough, a second probably wouldn't be either.

He needed to get up close and personal.

Ether crackled through his body when he activated his physical enhancements and sprinted toward the town. Danny didn't bother with his stealth field. Each stride gouged the earth when he pushed off. All that mattered was getting to the demon as fast as possible.

He bounded over the town wall like it was a hurdle and kept going.

Ten long strides brought him directly under the demon.

A tentacle lashed out at him.

Danny leapt, sliced ten feet off it, grabbed on, and started climbing. The other tentacles tried to knock him off. The ethersword made light work of them and soon it was raining chunks of demon flesh.

He reached the base of the tentacle and slashed through the demon's belly. His sword passed through it, doing nothing. It was like cutting through air.

Danny looked closer. The demon's body had no physical form. It was just a mass of corrupt energy. If he couldn't kill it, he'd have to dissipate it.

Wrapping himself in armor of divine energy, Danny yanked down on the tentacle and launched himself into the demon's body. As soon as he reached the center, he released a burst of power in every direction. The demon's essence resisted, but soon spears of divine energy burst out in every direction, reducing it to demonic Swiss cheese.

The corruption began to dissolve even as Danny started to fall.

A swirl of wind magic caught him and lowered him gently to the ground. Danny took a knee, breathing hard. That had taken a fair bit out of him.

"When the mistress said you were still alive, I admit I thought she was mistaken." Danny looked up to find the sexy nun headed his way, her black whip burning with hellfire. Pity he hadn't gotten her in the blast too. "I had great plans for this area, Hero. And now you've turned them to ruin. Still, if I kill you, the mistress will no doubt reward me well."

The whip snapped, sending a ball of hellfire streaking in at him.

Danny rolled out of the way and sprang to his feet. Ether flowed into him, but it felt sluggish. As he feared, he'd used too much power destroying the demon.

He sliced an incoming fireball in half, lunged, and swung the ethersword.

Her whip blocked his slash and they jostled back and forth, each trying to gain an advantage. His inability to overwhelm her with raw power told Danny all he needed to know about his current condition.

He jumped back, braced his foot, and lunged.

The nun spun away but hissed when his blade cut a shallow groove across her back.

Danny bore in, determined to press his advantage.

That decision nearly cost him. She evaded an overhead blow and countered with a snap of her whip. Danny jerked his head back but not quite fast enough. The very end of the whip burned a line down his right cheek.

Before she could recoil the whip, he stepped closer and punched her right in the face using the ethersword's hilt like brass knuckles. The force of the blow caved her skull in and she fell, unmoving, to the cobblestones. Evil or not, he couldn't help feeling somewhat ambivalent about smashing a woman's face in.

He barely had time to catch his breath before a chorus of groans caused him to spin around. A pack of five thralls was headed his way. Danny swallowed a groan of his own. All he wanted to do was rest. Instead he straightened and tightened his grip on the ethersword. The faster he dealt with these things, the better.

Before he could move, a sword burst out of the center thrall's chest. In a few seconds Lyra reduced them to unmoving lumps of flesh. Danny wasn't about to complain.

"You okay?" She sounded like she meant it. Then he remembered Lyra still needed him to seal the portals, so of course she wanted him alive.

"Fine, but tired. Whatever that cloud demon thing was, killing it was no easy task. Oh, you should know that the priestesses of Ardent Lilly have been warned I'm still alive. That seems like cheating, but I suppose she figured if Adonael could tell Eve the demon king survived, letting her team know the hero did as well is fair."

"It may be fair, but it's a problem. They'll be hunting for you." Lyra looked back over her shoulder. "There are a few more thralls that need cleaning up. You up for it?"

"Sure. And I think you're wrong. They won't be hunting

for me. The priestesses have their own plans. Assuming one per church, that's a lot of trouble wandering around." Danny put the ethersword away and drew his regular blade. It was plenty to deal with a few thralls.

Lyra's expression made it clear she didn't care for his thoughts. "You know, you have a way of saying the most awful things in the most casual way. I hope your theory is false, for all our sakes."

Danny hoped he was wrong as well, but he didn't think so.

CHAPTER 28

The mayor of Moreton, which was the name of the town near Morel Castle, wanted to thank Lyra, Eve, and Danny personally for preventing a far-worse catastrophe than what befell the town. While Danny appreciated the thought, he had no desire for his new persona to become famous. As far as everyone knew, Lyra had been the one to defeat the demons and he was happy to keep it that way. So instead of attending a stuffy ceremony, Danny found himself once more back in Castle Morel's courtyard.

He didn't know what he expected to find. And frankly, even if he found nothing, it was still better than attending the ceremony. When he explained his intentions to Lyra she'd looked jealous. When he asked why she didn't blow the whole thing off she replied that sometimes it was necessary to do things you didn't like for the good of the kingdom.

She hadn't sounded like she particularly believed what she was saying, but that was fine. Danny didn't care one way or the other.

Putting the pointless exercise out of his mind, he headed for the keep. In addition to searching for clues, he needed to destroy any bodies that remained behind. Someone was going to have to retrieve Alban and his knights as well, but that was another task which didn't interest Danny. Let the locals handle it. They were the ones stuck living under his rule.

A quick sweep of the first and second floors yielded nothing beyond a handful of bodies in need of destroying. Not that he'd expected to find anything. Any secrets would be downstairs where the spell circle had been.

He descended the steps and strode through the storage area and into the dungeon. As he feared, nothing remained of the circle. The remains of the people used to power the spell were also gone, consumed in the process he assumed. He walked around the chamber, studying the ground and the ether. Both were clean. Though a few wisps of corruption remained here and there, they didn't concern him.

When he'd made a full circle, he blew out a breath. There was nothing here and he was wasting his time. Lyra said they'd be leaving at first light to seal the next portal and that was fine with Danny. He'd already done more than he planned to on this mission. Not that it wasn't satisfying to rescue innocent people, he just felt like all this running around was keeping him from completing his real task.

He shook his head and walked toward the exit. Thinking that way was only going to get him in trouble. What little he'd learned about the summoning spell indicated that destroying the thing was apt to be the task of a lifetime. If he was getting frustrated now, what hope did he have of lasting to the end?

Halfway across the room Danny stubbed his toe on a

piece of stone jutting up a little above the floor. What the hell?

He grabbed the stone and pulled. A section of the floor lifted up. Underneath he found a black stone carved with red runes. Danny's Infernal was limited, but just looking at the stone was enough to tell him it was bad news. At a minimum, it wasn't the sort of thing he wanted to leave lying around.

A glowing aura of holy energy surrounded his hand and he bent to collect the black stone. As soon as he touched it, black sparks shot out, making his hand tingle. Definitely a good thing he took safety precautions. He stuck the stone in storage. It should be safe enough in a pocket dimension.

Looking back into the hole, he frowned. A strip of parchment was lying in the bottom. The writing on it was also Infernal. The few words he recognized talked about planting hell seeds. Was the stone some sort of seed? He shuddered to think what might grow from such a thing.

A final check of the room revealed nothing else of interest. Satisfied, Danny retraced his steps outside. Fresh air had never smelled so good. Time to head back to the inn. Maybe Lyra could tell him more about the stone and what the demons had planned.

○

Lyra couldn't begin to describe how much she despised official functions. Usually she could beg off, but the mayor insisted that he wanted to publicly thank her for defeating the demons. He was also grateful to Eve for protecting as many people as she did inside the temple of Adonael.

It was over now and the two women were on their way

back to the inn. They had about an hour until sunset. Daniel should have returned from exploring the castle. Lyra wasn't sure if she was hoping he found something or not. They certainly had enough to do without a fresh problem popping up.

Beside her, Eve's face was bloodless. The magic she'd used clearly took an even greater toll on her than Daniel's had him. It would be a wonder if she was in any shape to leave in the morning.

The priestess wobbled and Lyra put a hand on her shoulder. "Are you okay?"

"Fine, just tired. I think I'm going to sleep well tonight. Too bad Dan—uh, Ronin didn't want to join us. He really deserved most of the credit."

"Yes, but he doesn't want it. Drawing official attention would be a problem for him, as would explaining how a simple scout did what he did. Having him explore the castle and search for clues was the better option. I rather wish I could've gone with him instead."

"I could tell. I think you made the mayor nervous."

Lyra snorted. "I make most humans nervous. I no longer pay much attention to your reactions."

When they reached the inn, Lyra opened the door and guided Eve through. The priestess was nearly asleep on her feet. She debated carrying the woman, but dismissed the idea. It wasn't much further.

The few patrons watched them as they passed through the common room but no one spoke. Lyra ignored the curious gazes and kept moving. They reached the staircase and started climbing, slowly since it took all of Eve's concentration to manage each step.

At the top Lyra froze. An ethereal marker hung in the air

in front of Daniel's room. He must have found something. Something that couldn't wait until morning.

She glanced at Eve, whose eyes were closed and her breathing steady. Right, she could be filled in tomorrow. Lyra scooped her up, carried her to her room, and set her on her bed. Eve never even flinched.

With a little sigh of almost envy, Lyra made the short walk to Daniel's room. She knocked twice and he said, "Come in."

Daniel was seated on the edge of his bed, a book in hand. Lyra looked closer. It was the fourth volume of the History of the Elf-Blood People. So he did take the books out of Castle Villipan's library.

"Interesting reading?" she asked.

"Very. I can't decide if your people were more arrogant or cursed." He gestured at the small room's lone chair. "Take a load off."

She sat. "I assume you found something at the castle."

"You assume correctly, though exactly what I found is another matter. My host body has no memory of anything like it and I haven't read anything that described such a thing. Hold on."

He opened his pocket dimension, conjured a holy aura around his right hand, and reached in. A moment later he pulled out a black stone that made her want to retch just looking at it.

Her feelings must have shown on her face as he said, "That was my first impression as well. There was also a short note written in Infernal."

Daniel left the stone floating in midair surrounded by the protective aura and pulled out a strip of parchment that he passed over. Lyra grimaced when she touched it.

"What?" he asked.

"This is made from human skin."

"Great. Now I need to wash my hands again. Can you read it? I could only make out a few words." Daniel got up and went to the side table to wash his hands.

"'To whoever is reading this, know that you have only found one of the seeds of your destruction. The quadripartite resurrection cannot be stopped and I will return to claim this land in Ardent Lilly's name. Savor your last days of freedom as soon you will be slaves or food for the demons.' Signed the demon king."

"Well that's disconcerting." Daniel sat back down. "Does it mean anything to you?"

"Not much. The quadripartite resurrection must be the process by which the demon king was brought back to life. Though I have no idea what it entails. The stone is clearly the seed mentioned in the note, but what it's supposed to grow into I couldn't say."

"What do the runes on the stone itself mean? I recognized power and summoning, but that's not enough to figure out what it does."

Lyra beckoned and the stone seed floated over. Another gesture caused it to spin around so she could read the markings. "These are runes of power, not description. It's just darkness, power, and summoning over and over again, each time written by a different person. Fifteen different people all together."

Danny frowned. "How can you tell?"

"Just as everyone's handwriting is unique, all spellcasters inscribe runes with a unique style. My guess is that fourteen priestesses plus the demon king did this."

"So, does that mean there are thirteen more of these things lying around?"

"Maybe, but there might be more or less. It may have taken fifteen people to weave the magic, but that doesn't mean they could only make one for each person."

"What are you going to do about it?" he asked.

"You mean what are we going to do about it, don't you?"

"I mean what I said. One diversion was plenty. Once we seal the portals, I'm heading back to Rosenbar, getting my money, and seeing about joining that grand caravan Trevor mentioned."

Lyra didn't like her chances of finding all the seeds and defeating the priestesses with only Eve for help. And having seen what they'd be dealing with, calling in some weak human knights would only be dragging them to their deaths. She needed Daniel and that was all there was to it.

The problem was, she had no idea how to convince him. A moral argument from the person who stabbed you in the back of the head wasn't going to carry much weight.

"What do you want me to do with this thing?" He gestured at the stone.

"Put it back in your pocket dimension. I don't want to experiment too much while we're in town. If we trigger something, better we do it many miles from any people."

He nodded and put the stone away. "I almost forgot, what did you end up doing about Alban and his men?"

"I mentioned it to the mayor and he sent a team of guards to collect them. The temples will oversee removing their mind control spells."

"Fantastic, that's one thing we don't have to worry about. Nice when someone else handles a problem for a change, isn't it?"

Lyra nodded. She couldn't argue with him. "Was there anything else?"

He offered a weary grin. "Is that not enough?"

"More than enough, I just wanted to confirm before I returned to my room. Eve is already sound asleep and I'd say she has the right idea."

"See you in the morning."

Lyra took her leave, closing the door softly behind her. This demon king had them running in circles. She wished she had some brilliant plan that would see Villipan through this nightmare, but all her experience made no difference now. Muddling through like a human didn't please her, but in the end, what else could she do?

CHAPTER 29

At high noon a full day after leaving Moreton, Lyra reined in her horse in the center of a large field. Danny hadn't seen a single sign of life in hours. If something bad was going to happen with the black stone, this was the perfect place for it.

They dismounted and Lyra said to Eve, "Could you take the horses to the tree line and protect them and yourself with a barrier?"

"Of course," Eve said. "But what about you two?"

"I'll handle defense while Daniel tries to destroy the seed. Once you're a safe distance away, we'll begin."

Eve took the horses' reins and led them away. She looked glum. Despite having saved a bunch of innocent townspeople during the attack, Danny knew she thought of herself as more of a burden than a help. He wished there was something he could do about that, but her skills were what they were. No one could be good at everything.

"What are we going to try first?" Danny asked.

"Infusing it with holy energy seems like the best bet, don't you think?"

"Probably. If I'm going to do this, I want the hero's armor. Having a chunk of evil blow up in my face, even with your magic to protect me, isn't an appealing prospect."

Lyra stared at him.

"What? Is that a problem?"

"No, it's brilliant. I didn't even think of having you wear the armor. Talk about a blind spot. Hang on."

She took the armor out of her storage and helped him strap it on. It was just like old times, but Danny refused to let nostalgia get the better of him. He also made a point of putting the helmet on before letting her move behind him. How did the old saying go? Kill me once, shame on you; kill me twice, shame on me.

With his body encased in a mithril shell, Danny took the stone in his right hand. Next he started a loop of holy energy, sending it through the mithril to make it stronger, then finally he squeezed as hard as his physically enhanced body would allow. He kept it up until it felt like his arms were going to fall off.

At last he let out a gasp and opened his hand. The stone sat there, completely unharmed, mocking him. He hadn't put so much as a scratch in the surface to show he'd accomplished something.

"Well, that's disappointing." Danny held it out so Lyra could look. "What do you think?"

She looked closer, eyes narrowed. "As far as I can tell, it looks exactly the same. That should be impossible given how much energy you applied. Yet I can't deny what I see. If you can't destroy the stone, then no one in Villipan can."

"Then what do we do with it now?"

"Put it back in your pocket dimension for now. Maybe one of us will get a workable idea. Do you want to take the armor off?"

"Yes. I don't want anyone to see me and get the wrong idea." Daniel kept a close watch on Lyra as she helped him take the armor back off. Happily she didn't try anything.

"You know I need you to seal the portals," Lyra said. "Even if I planned to stab you again, I wouldn't do it until the mission is complete."

"That's very reassuring." Danny returned the stone to storage and waved to Eve. "But I don't trust you at all and that's never going to change."

When Eve arrived with the horses she said, "That wasn't a very energetic reaction. What happened?"

"Nothing." Lyra swung up into her saddle. "The magic didn't affect the stone at all. We might as well have thrown it in a lake for all we accomplished. Let's go, there's plenty of daylight left."

Eve looked at Danny as they rode along behind Lyra. "Is she okay?"

He shrugged. "No idea. I think she's feeling a bit overwhelmed by everything. The portals were bad enough, but now she's got these weird stones and a dead duke adding to the chaos. At the rate things are going, the demon king might not even need to return—the Five Kingdoms may end up nothing but ruins without her help."

"We won't let that happen." When he didn't reply Eve said, "Right?"

Danny shrugged again. "I'll see the contract through. Other than that, you're on your own."

Even as he said it, Danny knew he was lying to himself. He might intend to leave the Five Kingdoms to their fate, but when it came down to it, he'd help the people who needed him. Maybe it was a character flaw, but he'd never been able to walk away from trouble. It made him a good Marine and a bad mercenary.

By some miracle, they made it all the way to Fell Forest without meeting a single demon or monster. Danny wasn't sure if that was good luck or bad since wiping out a few more of the nasty things could only be a plus for the locals.

They dismounted at the edge of the dark woods and Danny asked, "Okay, so we brought horses this time. What are we going to do with them? Leaving them here is likely to end with them being eaten."

"There's a spell I can use," Lyra said. "It's a psychic spell and I don't like casting it even on animals, but it shouldn't do them any real harm. I would've had us walk, but it was a long trip this time and we don't have time to waste."

They removed all the horses' tack and stored it in Danny's pocket dimension. That done, Lyra brushed each of the horses on the forehead and the ether stirred around them. When she was finished, the horses ran off. They looked no different to Danny. No magical aura protected them and whatever the spell did to their brains, he couldn't see it.

"What was the point of that?"

"It's a recall spell. When I trigger it, the horses will come running back, immediately, no matter what else they might be doing at the time. They'll ignore any danger in their effort to comply. It's an absolute compulsion, which is why I hate it. They'll run right past a giant without hesitation. It's a good way to get them killed."

They were just horses, so Danny didn't think it was a big deal. Not being a complete fool, he kept his opinion to himself. "How sure are you that the church is nearby?"

"As sure as I can be based on the previous ones. We may need to search a little in either direction."

He nodded and the trio set out under the protection of one of Eve's barrier spells. A slight chill filled the air as they passed under the canopy. The corruption didn't seem as thick. Was that the result of closing a couple of the portals? Danny wasn't sure, but he liked to think so. It gave him a sense of having accomplished something. Sometimes it felt like no matter how much they did, it amounted to nothing.

As with their last visit to Fell Forest, this one stayed peaceful for two days before Lyra paused and said, "I sense a concentration of corruption not far ahead. I think it's the church, but it might be a powerful demon. Get ready."

Danny opened his storage and reached for the ether-sword. When he did, he noticed the stone vibrating. He barely had time to wonder what was going on before it flew out like a rocket.

"Shit! Lyra!"

"I saw it. Come on."

The trio sprinted after the stone. Danny jumped rocks and dodged limbs all the while making sure he didn't get too far ahead of Eve. Leaving her behind wasn't an option given how defenseless she was.

Fortunately the chase didn't take long. An evil church that looked like the others he'd seen waited in a clearing. The door was wide open and nothing defended it. If anyone cared that they were sealing the portals, they clearly had no intention of doing anything about it.

Inside, the stone hovered four feet above the portal. Black lightning crackled between them and glowing red fissures ran all along the stone.

"This doesn't look good," Danny said as he activated the ethersword. "Any ideas?"

Neither Lyra nor Eve said a word. Both women were staring, transfixed, at what was happening in the center of the church. The red light coming out of the stone grew brighter by the moment and the vibrations grew ever more intense.

Looked like the damn thing was about to explode.

He grabbed Lyra and Eve by their arms and dragged them back out of the church. As soon as they reached the edge of the woods he put the biggest tree he could find between them and the church and added a protective barrier just in case.

"What are you—"

Lyra's question was cut off by an explosion that shook the clearing.

When the dust cleared, Danny peeked around the tree. Where the church had stood there were a dozen of the lamprey-headed demons, ten hellhounds, and a succubus holding a black iron spear.

Well, now Danny knew where all the demons were.

CHAPTER 30

D anny didn't know how the demons appeared. That was a question for later. For now all that mattered was dealing with the creatures in front of him.

He ducked out from behind the tree he'd been using for cover and charged right into the gathered demons. Physical enhancement combined with a divine barrier served nearly as well for protection as mithril armor. He also added anti-psychic magic for the succubus. It helped that the foes arrayed before him, while formidable, weren't even close to the demon king.

His first blow took the head off of a lamprey demon. The weaker ones never bothered with weapons, instead seeming content with their claws, fangs, and magic. That worked out perfectly for Danny, since the ethersword could cut effortlessly through the demons' flesh and bones.

A pair of hellhounds leapt at him from the left and right.

Danny jumped back and swung an uppercut blow that took the front legs off the nearest one and the muzzle of the other. He didn't have time to finish them before a mob of five lampreys and four hellhounds charged him from all directions.

Holy energy, channeled through the mithril hilt, exploded outwards in all directions. His attackers had been burned away along with a few of the closer demons. Only the succubus remained unharmed. No doubt her black iron spear had offered some protection.

The beautiful female demon glared at him with bloodred eyes then snapped her wings open.

Danny had no intention of letting her get away.

He leapt, kicked off the head of a lamprey, crushing it to pulp in the process, and swung. She got her spear around in time to stop the blow, but the force of it sent her crashing back into the ground. Danny landed in front of her and the two of them faced off.

No words were spoken before the white blade of his ethersword hammered into the black iron haft of her spear. The clash was oddly quiet since the ethersword wasn't made of metal. His heavy breathing and the demon's snarls were the only sounds.

Danny wasn't sure how she managed it, but somehow the succubus kept up with him for the first few passes. The black spear was everywhere, though it never got close to cutting him.

At last, whatever power she was drawing on ran out and Danny drove the ethersword through her chest. Having no intention of making the same mistake twice, he promptly hacked her head off.

He spun only to find Lyra finishing off the last of the weaker demons. Danny sensed no other corruption in the area, besides the ambient aura that was always there. Looked like they'd won this round.

Danny extinguished the ethersword but kept the hilt in his hand. For now, caution was the word of the day. He strode over to Lyra, and Eve came running over from her hiding place. By some miracle they'd all come through the battle unscathed.

"Does anyone need healing?" Eve asked.

"I'm good," Danny said. "They were all low-level demons, though the succubus put up a pretty good fight. I can't figure out where they came from. Did the stone summon them through the church's portal?"

"No," Lyra said. "They were inside the stone. The portal's corruption triggered the magic that released them. Looks like the portal was sealed in the process. That's a nice bonus."

"How could all those demons fit inside the stone?" Eve asked.

Danny had been wondering that exact thing.

"Demons are corrupt energy given a physical form." Lyra sheathed her sword and looked back at the ruined church. "Having them turn back into energy is simple. The hard part is reforming their host bodies. That takes a great deal of power. The stone stores that power until something triggers it."

"Like the portal?" Danny asked.

Lyra nodded and turned back to face him. "Or the demon king's return. Can you imagine the chaos of that many demons suddenly appearing out of nowhere in fourteen different secure locations at the same time? The Five King-doms would fall in a day. We need to find the rest of them as soon as possible and destroy them."

"What about sealing the portals?" Danny asked.

"If the stones are linked to the portals, destroying the stones should seal the connected portal just like what happened here."

"Yeah, and if they're not, you'll still have the threat of the portals to deal with after I leave. And my contract is for sealing portals, not destroying demon stones."

Lyra scowled at him and Eve looked none too pleased either. It seemed he wasn't winning any friends. "I'll risk it," Lyra said. "The stones are the bigger risk. Help me deal with them and I'll sign your contract just as if we'd done the job stated. You get paid either way."

"That works for me," Danny said.

"Once the contract is complete," Eve said. "Can't we just hire you for a new job?"

Danny shook his head. "The grand caravan is leaving in the fall. I mean to leave with it. I'm willing to give you until the contract is complete or the leaves turn. After that, I'm gone."

"We may need more time," Lyra said.

"Then you'd best figure out how to locate those stones in a hurry."

CHAPTER 31

Lyra guided her mount down the main street toward Castle Villipan. Though she begrudged the time, she needed to speak with the king as well as confirm that there was no source of corruption in the castle. It shouldn't take more than a day and would give her a chance to visit the library. She'd seen a book on demonology there that had a spell she thought might be useful. She hadn't bothered to learn it the first time she read it since it dealt with corrupt magic and her elf blood made that an unpleasant prospect.

But she had no choice if they were going to complete the task before Daniel's deadline. His tone and expression made it clear that he meant what he'd said about leaving the kingdom in the fall. Lyra was in no position to blame him. All things considered, it was a wonder he was willing to do as much for them as he had been.

Daniel and Eve had decided to travel together to the town nearest where she suspected the next church would be. It was as good a place as any to start their search for the stones.

It was also south and east of Moreton, bringing them closer to the capital. Once Lyra finished here, it would only take a few days to join them.

When she reached the castle, she was surprised to find the gate wide open again. The squad of guards on duty had also relaxed a fair bit if their easy smiles and banter were any indication. They fell silent at once when they realized who was approaching.

The squad commander bowed. "Welcome back, Lady Shael. His Majesty will be pleased to see you."

"You all seem to be in a good mood. Is there a particular reason for that?"

"I suppose you wouldn't have heard since you've been in the field. The commanders haven't reported a demon encounter in weeks. The worst of the threat appears to be over. King Richard ordered all emergency security protocols to end and the wizards and priests to return. Everyone hopes life can get back to normal."

Somehow Lyra managed to keep her expression smooth and calm. "That's wonderful news. Excuse me."

She flicked her reins and rode up to the keep. What was Richard doing? Even if he didn't know about the demon stones, he couldn't possibly think the danger had passed, not after what happened in Moreton. She'd sent three birds south with the news. Was it possible none of them made it through?

Lyra shook her head and dismounted outside the keep door. Speculating was pointless. She'd find out when she made her report.

Inside, she found the castle in an uproar. Servants were running to and fro, their arms laden. Lyra grabbed an unburdened teenaged servant. "What's going on?"

The girl's pale-blue eyes widened when she realized who had grabbed her. "We're preparing for a banquet. His Majesty has ordered a celebration to commemorate our victory over the remnants of the demon king's army."

Lyra let her go, unable to believe what she'd just heard. They hadn't won anything yet. The demon king was still plotting somewhere, gathering her strength. The demon stones were still waiting for the right moment to explode into chaos. And for all they knew, dozens of towns might yet be under the control of Ardent Lilly's priestesses.

The idea that they'd won the war was, on its face, ludicrous. What was Richard thinking? The fact that she didn't know worried her as much as anything. But unlike some of the other mysteries she had to deal with, this was one she could sort out on her own.

Her magic guided her deeper into the castle, toward the royal suite. She couldn't sense any other members of the royal family nearby and that was fine. This wasn't the sort of conversation you wanted others listening in on.

As she got closer, the servants became fewer and fewer. She frowned. There was something strange about Richard's presence. Perhaps he'd ordered the arcane knights to add some sort of defensive magic to his suite. That would be remarkably sensible considering everything else he was doing.

When she knocked on the suite door she felt no new magic. Something else must be interfering with her tracking spell. "It's Lyra."

"Come in, come in. I got word that you'd arrived."

Inside, she found Richard seated at the dining room table facing her, a smile plastered on his face that didn't reach his eyes. The many new wrinkles and worry lines had been smoothed away and he seemed completely at ease.

"I understand a celebration is in the works."

Richard nodded. "Indeed. You know demon and monster attacks have dropped to an all-time low. No doubt thanks to your hard work as well as the hard work of the knights. Celebrating your victories is important for morale, don't you think?"

"Did you not get the letter I sent from Moreton? The reason the attacks have stopped is that the demons have been transformed into black stones. I suspect that the enemy priestesses have hidden them in key locations so we can be overwhelmed from within when the demon king returns."

"So you found the stones. That's disappointing. Still, I shouldn't be surprised given your talent. I'm going to need you to keep quiet about that detail. Wouldn't want to spoil the festivities."

Lyra reached for her sword. She'd heard enough. "Who are you and where's Richard?"

"You don't want to draw that sword. Bring her in."

The door to the king's bedroom opened and Queen Cecile came in with Tara in front of her, a black iron dagger at the girl's throat. Tears stained Tara's cheeks and the poor girl looked terrified.

"You dare threaten my granddaughter? I'll cut your heart out and feed it to the dogs. And where's Nora?"

"You're in no position to be asking questions," the fake king said. "Unbuckle your sword belt and set it on the ground. Your ring key as well. Wouldn't want you getting access to your pocket dimension and pulling out something unpleasant."

Lyra hesitated. If she gave up her weapons, even with her magic, she was doomed.

"I have no doubt you could do all sorts of terrible things to us," Fake Richard said. "But not before your sweet granddaughter's head hits the floor. Black iron weapons are terribly sharp after all."

Lyra ground her teeth, but in the end, if she didn't want to sacrifice her granddaughter, she had only one option: obey. She tossed her sword belt and ring on the floor. "Satisfied? You can let her go now."

"I hardly think so," the queen said. "Even without a sword, your magic is more than enough to cause us all sorts of problems. No, young Tara will be staying as our guest until the preparations for the ritual sacrifice are complete. The life force of a quarter elf-blood will make a fine offering. Think of all we can accomplish."

Queen Cecile's figure wavered and vanished, revealing the voluptuous body of a demon priestess. The vile woman grinned at Lyra and touched the black iron blade to Tara's neck, drawing a whimper.

"Leave her alone, damn you!" She took a step toward the priestess then stopped. Much as she wanted to kill the human with her bare hands, everyone present knew she couldn't.

"My private guards will escort you to the dungeon. Tara will live for as long as you behave yourself. Cause any trouble, and she'll be punished. Clear?"

"Yes."

"Couldn't you misbehave a little?" the priestess asked. "I imagine elf-skin gloves would be ever so soft."

Lyra didn't react to the woman's vicious remark. It was

cruelty for the sake of it. Pointless evil that perfectly encapsulated what it meant to worship a demon lord.

A few moments later the suite door opened again and six knights in kingdom armor that reeked of corruption entered.

"Take her to the deepest cell in the dungeon," Fake Richard said.

Her guards escorted her via seldom used back halls to the castle's second underground level. It was where the kingdom kept the most dangerous criminals and those they wanted to disappear but not kill. It didn't get much use and right now she sensed no other life forms on the entire level. Looked like she had the whole place to herself.

One of the guards shoved her into the rearmost cell, then slammed and locked the door. None of them ever spoke a word, either to taunt her or to ask questions. That was enough to confirm to Lyra they were some sort of bound demon, little more than automatons useful for fighting and following orders without hesitation.

She sighed when she sensed their corruption leave the dungeon. She really was on her own. As long as the demons had Tara she could do nothing.

Well, there was one thing: pray that Eve could convince Daniel to come to the capital and investigate why she didn't return. Hopefully she could do it before whatever ritual they were planning began.

AUTHOR NOTE

Hello everyone,

Well, Lyra certainly found herself in a tough spot at the end out book 2. While she probably deserves some kind of karmic payback, ending up in the hands of demon worshippers is a little much. Be sure to join me for book 3, The Fate of The Five Kingdoms, to find out how she makes out.

If you don't want to miss any of my new releases, deals, general news about the Etherverse, you can signup for my newsletter on my website.

www.jamesewisher.com

Until next time, thanks for reading,

James E. Wisher

ALSO BY JAMES E. WISHER

Summoned to Another Words and Forced to Fight The
Demon King

The Summoned Hero

The Birth of Ronin

The Fate of The Five Kingdoms

The Plague Lands

Elfhome

The 72 Demons

The Blood of Solomon

A Friend in Need

The Demon Masks

Hunt For The Devil Man

The Immortal Apprentice Trilogy

The War With Audin (Prequel Novella)

The Hunt For Revenge

The Army of Darkness

The Apprentice Reborn

The Soul Bound Saga

An Unwelcome Journey

Darkness in Tiber

Depths of Betrayal

The Complete Aegis of Merlin Omnibus

Other Fantasy Novels:
The Squire
Death and Honor Omnibus

The Rogue Star Series:
Children of Darkness
Children of the Void
Children of Junk
Rogue Star Omnibus Vol. 1
Children of the Black Ship
Children of The End

ABOUT THE AUTHOR

James E. Wisher is a writer of science fiction and Fantasy novels. He's been writing since high school and reading everything he could get his hands on for as long as he can remember.

www.ingramcontent.com/pod-product-compliance
Lightning Source LLC
Chambersburg PA
CBHW030536030726
47495CB00004B/1022